SHORT STORIES

Vol. I

Mysteries
Thrillers
Historical

Rich DiSILVIO

Published by DV Books, an imprint of Digital Vista, Inc.

Author's Website: www.richdisilvio.com

- - - - - - - - - - - - - - - - - -

Names: DiSilvio, Rich

Title: Short Stories: Mysteries, Thrillers, Historical / Rich DiSilvio

Description: New York, USA: DV Books, an imprint of Digital Vista, inc.

Identifiers: ISBN 978-0-9983375-4-8 (paperback) |
ISBN 978-0-9983375-5-5 (eBook)

Subjects: Short Stories | Mysteries, Thrillers | WWII | Short stories, American--History and criticism

Illustrations/Photos: 18

CONTENTS

The Night That Music Died

Prelude: The Flight Home

Jeff Nussbaum glanced at the photo of his wife, Amy, and his two grown children on his desk as he switched off the lights in his Manhattan office. They were always the last vision Jeff wished to see before leaving work. But of course that was *after* he made sure to gaze at and admire the eleven Gold Records and eight Platinum Records that decorated his cluttered wall. Posters of his star rappers, whom he had groomed, branded and tirelessly promoted, filled every square inch of what remained in his 420 square-foot office at Rappin' Records.

As Jeff descended in the elevator from the thirty-fourth floor he anxiously pulled out his yarmulke and placed it over his short, gray curly hair. Jeff shook his head, annoyed at himself. He was not religious by the Book, but Amy took Shabbat very seriously. This Friday, however, was very different. KrayZee, one of Jeff's top-charting rappers, and his manager, Lemmon Lang, had been busting his balls and tied him up for hours.

Jeff nervously glanced at his watch. It was five o'clock. He knew Amy probably already lit the two candles—representing the two commandments to *remember* and *observe*—and was now impatiently waiting for him so she could recite the blessing to officially commence the Shabbat before sundown.

Jeff plowed through the sea of pedestrians and quick-paced down the busy streets as he made his way toward Penn Station. Off to the west the October sun was already nearing sundown as its golden rays glittered off the tops of the glass and steel buildings that soared above him. Aiming to catch the five-fifteen to Forest Hills, Jeff cut down Thirty-ninth Street near Hell's Kitchen Flea Market and ran down the vacant alley, holding his skullcap in place with one hand and his black leather valise in the other.

Having lost his breath, Jeff slowed down, yet as he did, he heard footsteps behind him gaining in velocity and volume. As he spun around, his eyes widened with surprise, first with bewilderment, then with fear!

A dark-hooded figure bore down on him and struck him across the face with brass knuckles. Jeff's dislocated jaw rattled as he lost his footing and wobbled. The assailant then whipped out a black switchblade with a chrome skull head at the end and, in rapid succession, impaled Jeff in the stomach ten times. Jeff let out an awful groan as he spit out blood and fell into the gutter.

The assailant snickered. "Dat's cause I can't *stomach* ya!"

He then bent over and pulled Jeff's tongue out of his bloody mouth, and added, "And dis is to shut dat damn trap of yaws!" With that, the assailant sliced off Jeff's tongue and spat, "How you like dat, you white supremist piece a shit!"

Jeff lay in the gutter gurgling as blood rapidly filled his mouth. He held his mutilated and bleeding stomach with trembling hands and closed his eyes. Bright flashing visions of Amy and his children illuminated his mind like a strobe-lit music stage. Fear rattled his body as the precious visions of his beloved family swirled deeper and deeper into a dark and ominous pit.

Jeff opened his eyes and could barely see the blurry vision of a woman hovering above him, gasping in horror as she frantically dialed 911 on her iPhone. But Jeff knew it was too late. He could feel his blood gushing rapidly out of his mouth and stomach into the grimy gutter. Unable to speak, Jeff closed his eyes once more to cherish the fleeting images of Amy and his children, knowing he only had seconds left. He expelled a bone-chilling sob as the visions flickered, then faded to black, his quivering body and erratic heartbeat coming to a dead stop. Jeff Nussbaum was gone.

Episode 1: **The Call**

I'm Detective Tony Antonio, or as my dear buddies call me: Tony Tony, or Tony Squared, or as a few wiseasses say, Ant-nee. At five-ten I received the call from Captain John Smith about the homicide.

However, this particular call came as a horrific shock. Not that I haven't heard about gruesome killings, or witnessed disfigured corpses before, but because I knew Jeff Nussbaum. We grew up together on Long Island, in the small town of Seaford. Jeff was always a big dreamer. As teens back in the 70s we always got into arguments over which bands were greater, and he clairvoyantly envisioned the day when he would own a record label and promote bands that would hit the top of the Billboard charts.

Well, at that time we both imagined it would be rock n' roll bands. After all, so many rockers howled rock would never die. But it did in fact die. Or at least it waned significantly over the years, being confronted first by disco and heavy metal, then by pop boy bands, then alternative bands, then hip-hop and finally rap and girly pop. As this progression, or digression, took place, Jeff and I debated fiercely: he believing in the latter and I the former.

But what did I know? Jeff studied music, even going to Julliard and graduating with honors in classical music, of all things. While, admittedly, I was just a turn-on-the-radio listener, grooving to the rhythms and rhymes of rock, dancing to disco, or bopping my head to the pounding bass of rap music blaring out of boom boxes or gaudy pimp cars when I worked the beat as a cop in Brooklyn. I guess you could say I just went with the flow. Life was about change.

Meanwhile, Jeff appreciated bold innovators, like Black Sabbath and Jimi Hendrix, and especially sophisticated rock bands with classical inclinations, like Emerson, Lake and Palmer, Yes, Jethro Tull, and Pink Floyd. He said they had taken modern music to its apex, and was disheartened by the blaring decline of sophistication as other genres arose. He equated music's digression to that of the fine arts, stating how the traditional masters, from Da Vinci and Vermeer to Bouguereau, were overshadowed by the less technical impressionists, who in turn were supplanted by the archaic abstractionists, who truly drove Jeff nuts, as he chastised them as being a bunch of talentless trilobites.

Yet, Jeff was also pragmatic. His father, Jacob, was a very successful trial lawyer, and although Jacob was initially disappointed that his son refused to follow in his lucrative footsteps, he eventually came around to it, being that *he* soon followed his son's lead and became an entertainment attorney once Jeff made millions with his renowned Rappin' Records label.

But the depressing task of going down into the morgue to view my old buddy's body brought all those fanciful memories to a screeching halt. As I viewed his bluish-gray corpse I gagged. The ten lacerations to his stomach and disfigured face, with missing tongue, were not only visually gruesome, but the raw emotions that ran through my veins shook me to the core. Despite Jeff's often outspoken nature he was a gentle, good-natured soul who cared passionately about his work, loved his family, and helped anyone in need. And that wasn't because I was his friend; the same was said by anyone who ever met Jeff. Well, not everyone, obviously. This homicide didn't add up. There are plenty of managers and producers in the music industry who were cutthroat shysters, deserving of a good beating or worse, but Jeff floated above those foul specimens like an owl over a sleazy flock of ravenous vultures.

Having first stopped by his house to console Amy and their two college kids, I then made a beeline to his office the next morning. I had requested that Jeff's employees meet there to answer questions, being that it was a better venue than the precinct, which offered no clues.

As I scanned Jeff's office I turned toward Jeff's A&R guy, named Gill Roberts, who looked about half my age, and asked, "So tell me, Gill, Jeff always made it home for Shabbat on Fridays, so why was he delayed last night?"

Gill shook his head dejectedly. "Not sure, Detective. We all left at two o'clock yesterday, well before he did."

I squinted. "Do you always cut out early on Fridays?"

"No, sir. Jeff told us all to go home early." Gill choked up, then added, "To get rest for the big day today."

"What big day?"

Gill pointed to a chair. "Do you mind if I sit?"

"No, of course not," I replied, as Gill wearily sat down and swallowed hard.

Gill looked up at me, then gazed at a poster on the wall. "See that?" he said as he turned back toward me.

"That's Headstorm; a new progressive rock band that Jeff was premiering tonight at the Garden."

I sat on Jeff's desk and peered at the poster. It featured a surrealistic image of a man's head with a tornado of thoughts blowing outward, revealing a beautiful vista with waterfalls, flowers, and futuristic buildings, while on the horizon were ominous storm clouds and lightning bolts. The apocalyptic storm was ravaging a rundown urban cityscape as the sun's rays spotlighted the utopian foreground.

"Intense!" I said.

Gill managed to smile, but only for a moment. "Yes, it is. It was Jeff's dream you know."

My lips twisted as I rubbed my chin and looked closer at the image of the man's face. It certainly wasn't an exact portrait of Jeff Nussbaum, but I did notice some subtle similarities.

I blinked hard. "Are you saying Headstorm is Jeff's band?"

Gill grasped a photo off the desk and handed it to me. "Not officially. These are the band members: Billy, Steve, Don, and Rick, but Jeff writes all their music and lyrics."

I glanced at the photo, but my eyes veered quickly back to Gill. "That's amazing." I scratched my head. "You see, I grew up with Jeff. We stayed in touch occasionally, but I know he always loved progressive bands. Yet I think he missed his chance by a few decades. And let's face it, he's made his millions by promoting rap artists with this label."

Gill nodded. "Yes, he did. But a year ago he had an epiphany. That's when he began writing the music for this new album. He knew he was too old to play and tour with the band, so he had us scout out talent, and—" Gill pointed to the photograph, "there they are: Headstorm."

Suddenly *my* brain was engulfed in my own head storm. *Why did Jeff think he could bring progressive rock back now?* I thought. *The world had changed. Kids today have far less attention span, being barraged by all sorts of media on multiple platforms, and wanting instant gratification. Progressive music is too long and dense.*

I looked at Gill. "Did Jeff really think he could pull this off? I mean, bring progressive rock back from the dead?"

Just then a young man with long hair in a ponytail and wearing torn jeans walked in. "Yes," he interjected. "Jeff had been frustrated for years and felt it was time to change things. In a word—revolt. My name is Barry Gottlieb, Detective. I was Jeff's personal assistant."

"Revolt, indeed," I said as I glanced at Jeff's cluttered walls, all filled with posters of various successful rappers. "And what did *they* think about Jeff's change of direction?"

As Gill and Barry twisted their lips and shrugged, I added, "I imagine it didn't go over too well."

"Not really," Barry said.

"You can say that again," Gill chimed in.

I looked back up at all the posters and pointed at them in a sweeping fashion. "Well, this makes for a great line up. So tell me, which one of these fine fellows would have a hard-on for Jeff?"

Gill pointed to a poster featuring a mean-looking thug, decked out in black leather pants, a gold sequin shirt, four gold necklaces, gold-plated sunglasses and gold teeth, and said, "Black Bullion. He got mighty pissed when Jeff decreased the budget for his latest album."

Barry nodded. "He sure did, but you should have heard KrayZee on the phone yesterday. Talk about pissed."

I turned to scan the posters to find this KrayZee fellow when Barry pointed behind me. "He's over there."

As I turned, my eyes landed on KrayZee's face. It was gnarly, mean, and filled up the entire poster. He was making a crazy twisted face and flashing his large silver teeth that were filed into sharp fangs. Clutched in his teeth was a black switchblade with a chrome skull's head at the base.

That image certainly didn't help exonerate him in my mind, as I said, "You boys do know that Jeff was repeatedly stabbed to death by some sort of a knife, don't you?"

They both nodded gloomily, as Barry said, "Yes, we got the low down from officer Kelley on the phone this morning."

Gill stood up. "Detective Antonio, let me just say…most of these guys are rough dudes, so just because KrazyZee has a knife between his teeth doesn't mean he's guilty."

I chuckled my mind-numbing thoughts away as I replied, "Yes, I know, Gill. I'm not convicting anybody solely on the premise of a photo." As my eyes swept across the colorful array of posters, each featuring one rough-looking rapper after another, I added, "Many of these bad boys are just putting on a theatrical show. But some are gangstas, *real* gangsters. So as far as I'm concerned, they're all suspects. Especially since they all had motives with Jeff's new direction. I imagine they all faced budget cuts, yes?"

"Well, most did," Barry replied. "A few haven't been receiving all that much attention due to their poor sales or rookie status. So I doubt they had motives."

"You can never be sure, Barry," I said. "They may have been disgruntled for being overlooked, since Jeff's big stars were getting all the attention and funding. Envy and jealousy can make some people do horrible things."

"Hmm, I guess you're right," Barry said. "I didn't look at it that way." He walked over to a filing cabinet. "So do you want the contact info for everyone on the roster, Detective?"

"For now I'll start with just Black Bullion and KrayZee. From what you boys told me, and the size of their posters, I suspect they're the two biggest acts you have. Am I right?"

"Yes, sir," Gill replied. "Those two would be my first choice as well."

I smiled. "Well, I hope you guys don't think you're excluded from this little round up."

Both their faces turned pale, seeming to glow pure white, especially in comparison to all the black faces on the walls.

Barry stuttered, "W-why would *we* have a motive? We loved Jeff like a brother…actually, like a father."

Gill added, "Yeah, you don't seriously think *we* had anything to do with it, do you?"

I pulled out a pad from my inner coat pocket and began writing as I said, "Although the woman who was the only witness said the perpetrator appeared to be a large black male wearing a black hoodie, I will need your home phone numbers and addresses boys. No one is exempt at this time, even though you're not at the top of the list. Black face paint can go a long way. So I'll thank you boys for your cooperation."

Episode 2: **First Suspect**

As I traveled on the Metro-North along the Hudson River I jotted down notes in my pad. No, not an iPad, I'm old school, pen and paper works just fine. And just for the record, I truly didn't suspect Gill or Barry, their alibis checked out anyhow, but its one of my darker pleasures: I like to scare the dickens out of some people, and Gill and Barry seemed like good fodder to play a prank on. I never said I was an angel!

But I did call them prior to hopping on the train to let them know they were off the hook, so who knows, maybe they'll thank me, since a good scare does work like a laxative to clear the system out. And kids these days are into that whole organic cleansing crap.

Anyhow, I arrived at Black Bullion's home, or should I say *villa,* at one o'clock that afternoon in Ossining, New York. His gated estate was a sprawling oasis of manicured property nestled in the woods with a distant view of the Hudson River.

Parked in the huge circular driveway were two black limos and a rare 1958 Ferrari 250 Testa Rossa, all with solid gold grills, gold mag wheels, and glittering gold accessories.

As I exited the rickety yellow cab, Black Bullion approached me.

I looked up at him. He was massive, much bigger than his photo in the poster, appearing like a wall of solid meat and muscle, with bulging veins that protruded out of his beefy biceps and forearms.

"Do I call you Black, Bullion or what?

"BB be fine," he said with a stone-cold expression.

"Well, BB, I'm sure you know why I'm here."

"Yeah, I knows, I saw da news, Bro," he said with a twitch of the head and a downward thrust of his hand. "I gots me an eighty-five inch LED flat screen. And a helluva lot more, too."

I glanced at his mansion, then at his 16 million dollar Ferrari and gilded limos, and shook my head. "How the hell does someone like *you* amass all this wealth just for singing, or rather *speaking*, vile songs?"

I expected my antagonistic overture to elicit a snarled response or even a punch to my face, but Mr. Bullion laughed. "That's what is so grand about living in America, Detective Antonio," he said in perfect English.

Startled, and with my test foiled, I said, "Do you mean to say your whole image is a gag?"

"Of course, Detective. I graduated from Marist College, as did fellow alumni Bill O'Reilly. But that old geezer graduated long before I did." His eyes scanned me from head to toe, then zeroed in on me, as he added, "And

I'll bet with that cocky attitude of yours you're a fan of that blowhard."

Now *I* laughed. "Not exactly. He may have some lucid thoughts but his megalomania clouds the picture."

"Well, I have no clouds to ruin my *true* picture," BB said. "It's only on stage as Black Bullion that I perform like one of those hoodlums over there." He pointed toward the Hudson River, which was visible through a large aperture in the woods.

As I squinted I could vaguely see the large Sing Sing correctional facility along the shoreline down below. I smiled. "Yes, you do. You *sing sing* some vile lyrics, BB. Why do you do it?"

Bullion's plump black face withered into a solemn expression of grief. "My brother is still incarcerated in Sing Sing, Detective. We were just kids at the time, and Leon got mixed up with some bad dudes, drugs, and criminal escapades. It literally killed my mother to see him in prison and my pa has become melancholy and distraught. I had this mansion built so I could look after my father and keep an eye on my little brother. I visit him daily. It's crucial that I keep his spirits up." Bullion shook his head. "I hired the best attorney I could find, but it's been seven years and still no progress. Hopefully, one day. Who knows?"

I swallowed hard. "I'm sorry, BB. That's a tough card to be dealt."

An odd moment of silence fell between us. It was finally broken when I asked, "But, tell me. Why the gangsta image and vile lyrics?"

Bullion smiled. "Wayward kids gravitate to the devil, Detective, not to saints. I needed a hook. As for my lyrics, they may express the gangsta lifestyle prevalent in black communities, but they always end on a positive note, unlike my peers. I sing of the transition from street gangsta to rich rap artist or professional basketball player and so on. Good messages. Yet the press only fixates on my nasty words."

"I must admit," I said, "I listened to a few of your songs on the way up on my daughter's iPod, but never the whole song, being disgusted by the degrading first few lines."

Bullion gazed at me like a college professor. "That's why it's imperative to read an entire book or listen to an entire song, Detective, if you plan on being a valid critic. You, of all people, should know that."

My chest deflated. "You're absolutely right, BB."

"The name is Brian, Detective, Brian Bowden, in case you want to know the truth."

I smiled. "Yes, BB, I mean Brian, I always want to know the truth. So what can you tell me about Jeff Nussbaum? Did he make a lot of enemies, with you or anyone else?"

"Listen, Jeff was a great guy, Detective. He had a sincere desire to make whatever or whomever a success when he committed to it, yet he did anger quite a few people. Let's face it, anyone in a position of power and wealth always has enemies, as well as loyal advocates."

"Very true. So where do *you* stand, Brian?"

"Let's just say I'm a disappointed advocate. Jeff made me the star I am, which as you can see—" he swung his arm around, pointing to his posh mansion and expensive toys, "I have no complaints and owe him for making my dream a reality. But his obsession with his new mission stepped on a lot of toes, mine included. But kill him, never! I worked too hard to get to where I am, and with my brother as an example of foul thinking and foolish actions, I could never jeopardize my father and brother's well being that way."

I looked deep into Brian's eyes, and said, "Can I trouble you for a favor?"

"Sure, anything," he replied sincerely.

"Can you drive me to the station? I'm done here."

Episode 3: **Second Suspect**

I headed back to Manhattan and arrived at KrayZee's exotic penthouse, which overlooked Central Park. It was three-thirty and the October air was brisk but comfortable as I entered the building. Taking the elevator to the top floor, I entered KrayZee's lavish penthouse. It was decorated with white Carrara marble flooring, white Italian leather couches, a huge Jackson Pollack painting on one wall and a series of three huge portraits of KrayZee on another wall, all in various techniques: one ala Warhol, another ala Picasso, and one ala Horace Pippin.

I stood by the large wall of windows that offered a panoramic view of Manhattan. It was spectacular. Down below I noticed a speeding EMT truck rushing to the scene of some calamity with its flashing lights and sirens blaring. I turned to scan KrayZee's upscale furnishings once again, then bulleted him with my antagonistic test. "How is it that a thug like *you* makes millions just for speaking despicable words, while EMTs, who save people's lives, get paid squat?"

KrayZee's face wrinkled as he gritted his teeth and snapped, "I be an artist! Dat's why!" He pointed to his cherished painting—Pollack's huge canvas splattered with drips of paint. "You see dat? Dat's art, man. Dat's timeless shit, like my muzik. You ain't gonna see no EMT given da world art. Dey may help a handful, but I inspya millions! So I make da millions! You dig, bro?"

Before I could respond, KrayZee's manager, Lemmon Lang, entered the room and said, "He's right, you know. You may not comprehend the value of true art, Detective, but KrayZee represents modern America. His lyrics resonate with the masses because they're true. Honest and timeless, as they depict the oppressed world that the white man has thrust blacks into."

I snickered. "Mr. Lang, the white man has been blamed for too many things for far too long. With Johnson's affirmative action back in 1965, blacks have infiltrated just about every field of endeavor, fairly and unfairly, and have risen to respectable heights. They've been given more opportunities than all other races. After all, how did Obama manage to get elected? It was by the golden college opportunities afforded him and by the good will and votes of white Americans." I glanced at KrayZee, and added, "And how did your artist here become a millionaire? Did white men hold him down? No. I think Jeff Nussbaum was critical to his success, wouldn't you agree?"

Lang laughed. "Jeff was just a mere financier. KrayZee's talent is what made him the star he is today. All of Jeff's money is worthless without a true talent to promote."

"Well, I knew Jeff personally. We were childhood buddies, and I know his philosophy ran counter to your skewed interpretation of what an artist really is."

As KrayZee snorted like a pit bull and cracked his neck, agitated, Lang motioned to him to calm down, while he responded, "Detective, the white man is just jealous and infuriated that blacks have given America its true voice. From jazz to blues and now hip-hop and rap, we blacks have dominated the music field. Our African jazz even gave birth to the white man's rock n' roll."

Thoughts of Jeff's many heated lectures about music came screaming back into my head as my mouth went on autopilot, "Mr. Lang, as Jeff once told me, African Americans often blow their horn about how they invented jazz, however, the fact is, their African musical roots consisted of primitive war drums and archaic animal horns. They never stop to realize how fortunate they've been to utilize the white man's many musical inventions; from the pianos they play to the saxophones and trumpets they blow, to the basses, cellos and guitars they strum; in essence, all the necessities to make great music."

As Lang and KrayZee gazed at me, mute, my mouth continued, "And for your information, jazz did not appear out of a vacuum or solely out of black communities. The roots of jazz also evolved out of European classical music. One only needs to listen to composers at the turn of the twentieth century to see how Franz Liszt was the first to compose atonal, dissonant music in the 1800s, which laid the seeds for a string of composers afterwards as well as white leaders of marching bands in America, like Jack Laine in New Orleans, whose jazzy tunes were instrumental in influencing blacks and giving them a start, thus leading to jazz and even rock many years later. But those not versed in the full breadth of music history take it upon themselves to sing a different tune, one filled with falsehoods."

Lang and KrayZee gazed at me, stunned. My rebuttal was unexpected, even by my standards, as I realized I had basically parroted Jeff's words from so many years ago from memory. I felt as if Jeff entered my soul to lambaste his offenders, or could it be murderers? My curiosity and suspicions became more acute as I turned toward KrayZee and asked, "Now getting down to business. Where were you last night between four and five o'clock?"

KrayZee gazed at Lang for instruction, as his master replied for him, "KrayZee was with me, right *here* having cocktails."

I turned toward Lang. "*Cocktails.* Really? What kind?"

Lang hesitated, then uttered, "Uh, Limoncello… on the rocks."

I didn't like either of their shifty eyes or Lemmon squirt's suspicious Limoncello answer.

I looked at the poster of KrayZee, which he had framed and hanging over his gas-fired fireplace. "That's a brazen photo you have there. Or perhaps I should say incriminating photo."

"What the hell are you getting at!?" Lemmon demanded, as KrayZee took a bold step forward and flexed his muscles.

"A witness indentified a large black man wearing a hoodie as the perpetrator. And as you probably know by now, Jeff was murdered with a knife." I glanced at KrayZee, then back up at the poster. "So, how do you explain that switchblade clenched between your teeth?"

KrayZee squinted. "I ain't gots no switchblade. Dat wuz a prop."

Lang stepped closer. "Yes, Jeff supplied that knife. I was there for the photo shoot. Feel free to ask anyone about it. In fact, Jeff had that knife custom made, its one of a kind. So there goes your baseless accusation, Detective, right out the window!"

I turned and glanced at the Manhattan skyline, as thoughts of tossing *their asses* out the window clouded my judgment. I was too close to Jeff and this case. My emotions were getting the better of me. I took a deep breath. I looked back at Lemmon Lang and KrayZee, feeling as if I were going a little *craZy* myself. I needed time to think. Fortunately, Lang gave me the exit initiative I sought, as he said, "Listen, Detective, if you have no further questions, we're finished here. We have to get ready for tonight's show."

I looked at KrayZee. "Oh, where are you playing?"

Lang stepped in front of him and pointed toward the door. "At the Garden. Now please go."

"Just a minute," I said. "Headstorm is playing there tonight."

Lang smirked. "No, they cancelled. We're taking their place."

"Why did…or rather, how did you manage that?"

"Because I'm a manager, Detective. I *manage* things. Now please, go! KrayZee needs to rest."

"Very well, good luck tonight," I said as I took my leave.

Episode 4: **The KrayZee Gig**

I arrived at Madison Square Garden at eight o'clock. I waved my badge and slipped into the auditorium. The stage was lit up with flashing colored lights while dry-ice vapor billowed. Meanwhile, the loud, pounding thumps of electric drums rattled the walls and my entire ribcage. The audience was oscillating to the rapping rhythms of KrayZee's crazy lyrics while the smell of marijuana, and God knows what else, wafted through the air.

Diligently, I made my rounds to question all the security guards to see if they knew anything about KrayZee or even Jeff, but I hit a dead end. A bit discouraged, I then decided to listen to KrayZee's gig to see what the crazy thug's *gig* truly was. I walked to the back of the auditorium and came upon a Hispanic security officer in his thirties, named Héctor.

He looked at me and smiled. "What is a guy like *you* doing *here*?"

"Why?" I said. "I see a few white people in the audience."

Héctor laughed. "Yes, but they're all twenty-year-old kids. What's *your* deal, papa?"

"Okay, first of all, I'm only fifty-eight." Eliciting a laugh, I then pulled out my badge.

Héctor smiled and pulled out a set of earplugs. "Care for these?"

"Thanks," I said as I popped them in my ears.

The muffled sound was a godsend. "I don't know how these musicians don't go deaf," I said.

"Do you really call this rap crap music?" he said.

I laughed. "So what kind of music do *you* listen to? Salsa?"

He smiled. "Well, Salsa when the wife and I want to dance, but when I'm alone, it's always classical."

I recoiled. "Really? Classical? You seem a bit too young for that, *sonny boy*."

Héctor laughed. "Perhaps. It's just that classical music isn't given a chance these days. As far as I'm concerned, music has gone down the drain." He turned and looked at the stage. "Look at that. It's sinful. Yet they get all the attention, funding, and stardom. How can simplistic garbage like that ever compare to a symphony?"

"I wouldn't know," I said. "I never listened to a full symphony, only excerpts. And I've learned that you can't pass judgment about music without knowing all the details first."

Héctor smiled. "*Sound* advice." As I chuckled, he continued, "But I've listened to all these rappers while working here and classical, so here's *my* educated critique, Detective. A rap musician plays three chords for a thousand people while a classical musician plays a thousand chords for three people." As I mulled that over, he added, "But I also came to realize that sophisticated music is not for the simple-minded masses. That's why there was only one Einstein, one Tesla, one Leonardo, one Tchaikovsky and so on. If brilliance were the norm, Detective, imagine where mankind would be today."

I rubbed my chin. "Interesting thought," I said as I glanced back up at the stage.

KrayZee was bopping around doing some primitive animalistic-like dance as the crowd roared and mimicked his every move. I gazed back at Héctor. "Well, at least the simple masses are enjoying themselves."

Héctor rolled his eyes. "Yes, if you can't enlighten them with brilliance appease them with bullshit. So, let them chant and dance to their primal orgy as civilization crumbles. What the hell, after all, that's where we're all headed."

"Well, *this* rap music may be primitive," I said, "but what about Miranda's play, *Hamilton*? I hear it's rather complex and features quite a bit of history. Not to mention it being a huge success."

Again Héctor rolled his eyes. "Really? You mean to say you were sucked in by that nonsense too?"

I squinted. "What do you mean?"

"Look, I'm Hispanic and love my people and culture, but Miranda's play is the ugliest form of racism there is. Alexander Hamilton and all the founders were white, yet he strictly demands an all Latino and black cast, except for the villain, who just so happens to be a white man. Meanwhile the lyrics are filled with innuendos. It's bigoted propaganda. Yet, because the media has always been an advocate for revisionist history they too openly embrace and laud it. They're hypocrites, all of them. They preach diversity and equality yet push racist tripe like *Hamilton* onto a public that is either ignorant of their anti-white agenda or disgruntled racists who seek revenge for ancient ills. Either way it gets rave reviews and slyly conditions unsuspecting minds."

Héctor glanced back up at the stage. "Look, the truth is, I really don't mind that rappers like KrayZee cater to the simple minded, or that new genres arise that are less complex. Different people have different capacities and different tastes. But that the power mongers with money and clout ram it down everyone's throat to the exclusion of almost all other forms of music is not only grossly unfair, it's an utter travesty." Dejectedly, he gazed back at the stage, shaking his head as his lips twisted.

Suddenly I found myself thinking about Jeff's failed attempt to reverse what he saw as the downfall of music and culture. I was beginning to understand and appreciate his valiant effort, and I now viewed his death in a different light. It was actually the night that music died. All hope was now lost. A veil of melancholy came over me. But then I recalled Don McLean's song *American Pie,* where he honored the deaths of Buddy Holly, Richie Valens and J.P. Richardson who died in a plane crash in 1959. And like that dreadful moment, my only hope now was that music would experience a rebirth somehow from someone with Jeff's talent, ambition, and financial means so that his death wouldn't have been in vain. After all, rock n' roll continued after the deaths of those early pioneers, so perhaps there was a chance for rock or progressive music to thrive once again.

I waved to Héctor to exit the arena so we could talk further. As we entered the lobby, I removed my earplugs. "So, do you know anything about this KrayZee fella?"

"Sure do. He was a street punk that got arrested several times for petty larceny and drug dealing, but his friend, Lemmon, always managed to bail him out. Lemmon saw something in him and directed him towards music. Naturally he became his manager and the rest is history."

I rubbed my chin. "What's the deal with this Lemmon Lang character?"

Héctor pulled a Snickers bar out of his pocket and waved it. At first I thought he was signaling that Lang was nuts, but then realized he was just offering it. I refused and he took a bite and replied, "From what I've heard, Lemmon was a street hustler. Street savvy but also educated. And very money hungry."

A young male approached Héctor and asked where the restrooms were. Héctor directed the youth, then turned back toward me and said, "In fact, Lang was here yesterday arguing with the director and tongue-lashing Jeff."

"What about?" I queried.

"Money, of course, and scheduling. It seems he wanted this evening's event to be for his golden goose, rather than for Jeff's new white band." He pointed to one of the remaining posters for Headstorm that wasn't covered over with a KrayZee one, and added, "Things got pretty hot.

In fact so hot that I had to physically drag Lemmon out the door before fists were thrown. Lang was in Jeff's face, ramming his finger in his chest and calling him the Grand Dragon."

I squinted. "Grand Dragon? What does that mean?"

"The Grand Dragon was the name given to a leader of the Ku Klux Klan."

I paused a moment as I thought about Héctor's comments; namely, how Lang's scathing remarks to Jeff were fueled by irrational racial hatred and how Héctor said *disgruntled racists seek revenge for ancient ills.* I also found myself thinking about Lang's earlier statements to me, which at the time I thought were typical ramblings about the supremacy of jazz and black music by a proud black man. But evidently, Lang harbored an intense hatred and Aryan-like belief in racial superiority that now sent a shiver down my spine. Someone with intense loathing had viciously mutilated Jeff, and Lang's modus operandi was now coming sharply into view.

I gazed at Héctor. "I think I've been focusing on the wrong guy. This Lemmon Lang seems like a psychotic powder keg. What time did that altercation occur?"

"Around two o'clock or so."

"Thanks, Héctor!"

I left the building and phoned headquarters. I asked for a team to meet me at the crime scene. I caught a cab and arrived moments later. The team was already there, and I said, "Check every dumpster and sewer grating from here to the nearest bus stop or Metro station. I suspect Lang ditched the knife before heading home. And get sanitation down here to open them up and crawl through that slop if need be. I want to find this damned knife!"

Five hours passed as I paced up and down the street sipping on a cup of Joe, while ugly thoughts of Jeff lying in the gutter plagued me. Then I heard a yell, as a sanitation worker ran up to me, a big smile plastered on his dirty face. "Detective Antonio, I found a switchblade! It was tossed down the sewer two blocks from here."

"Don't handle it too much," I prompted as I grasped the knife gingerly at the edge with two fingers. "I need to get fingerprints off this nasty demon." As I took a good look at it I recoiled! It was a black switchblade with a chrome skull's head at one end. "Jesus Christ!" I exclaimed. "Its Jeff's knife."

Carefully, I placed it in a Ziploc bag and thanked the sanitation worker.

I then brought the knife back to headquarters where they dusted it for fingerprints. And as sure as the dead skull on the knife we found Lemmon Lang's deadly fingerprints.

Episode 5: **The Pick Up**

The next evening I darted back to Madison Square Garden just as KrayZee's Sunday show was wrapping up. I gained access backstage and waited patiently, having a sudden desire to devour Lemmon Meringue pie.

As KrayZee entered backstage Lemmon emerged from the shadows. As he congratulated his cash cow I walked up and said," I need to speak with you, Mr. Lang."

Lemmon looked at me with dagger eyes. If looks could kill I'd be in the morgue alongside Jeff.

I said, "I'd like you to accompany me down to headquarters. I have a nice little switchblade I'd like to show you."

The daggers in Lemmon's eyes morphed into handcuffs. It was clear to see his thoughts, despite his vain attempt to conceal his guilt with a cocky, half-assed smile.

I left him struggling to maintain his stupid grin as long as I could. I like to see vipers squirm. After all, I did say I'm *no* angel.

After an odd tense moment, Lemmon caved in, his cheery cheeks wilting into a frigid frown. Unconvincingly, he said, "So, you found a knife. Is that supposed to concern or frighten me, Detective? I have an alibi, remember?"

I sniggered. "You're like a diaper, Lemmon…self absorbed and full of shit! We have your fingerprints. And another witness emerged, a worker from the Hell's Kitchen Flea Market. You're going *down!*"

Lemmon's eyes shifted as his chocolate cheeks turned cherry red. Unexpectedly, he made a dash for the exit.

I pulled out my Glock and gazed over at KrayZee, who immediately raised his hands. "I gots no problem wit ya, boss!"

"Very well, just stay put," I demanded.

Epilogue

My young partner, Bobby Moran, had been stationed outside by the exit and apprehended Lemmon Lang, who we escorted to headquarters for booking. It was later revealed during the trial that Lemmon altered his voice during the stabbing in case any witnesses overheard him. His vain attempt to appear like one of Jeff's rappers was compounded by the fact that he never expected Jeff's knife, which he had stolen, to be retrieved from the sewer. Fortunately there hadn't been rain for many days and the sewers were dry; his fingerprints left nicely intact. And with the new witness firmly identifying him, Lemmon's future didn't look too *fruit*ful, in fact it looked pretty *sour*.

Thirteen days after New Year's Day, Lemmon Lang was charged with murder in the first degree and shipped upstate to Sing Sing, where he now sits. Oddly enough, Lang was placed in Leon Bowden's old cell, being that Black Bullion's attorney managed to get Leon released.

Having stayed in touch with Héctor, I invited him to Rappin' Records, where Jeff's son, Daniel, decided to take over his father's business. As it turned out, Héctor not only loved classical music but also enjoyed composing music. He gave up his security job and became the official composer for Headstorm.

This case, and its KrayZee chain of events, proved to be a real head storm, all right. Yet I was deeply moved by the touching stroke of fate that emerged, for although human and music evolution doesn't always bring advancements, it appears sophisticated music didn't die that night after all. For, quite mysteriously, Jeff Nussbaum's luminous dream was given life from his dying breath.

The Death Ray Mystery

Pensively, I gaze at the casket of one of our century's most brilliant men as I sit numb and crestfallen in the Cathedral of St. John Divine in Manhattan, oblivious to the priest's hollow words that could never do justice to the neglected genius whose loss to humanity is incalculable.

Outside, the frigid January wind howls, aptly mirroring the cold rigid body lying within a cold wooden box that stands before a cold marble altar. The coffin sits stagnant, unlike the man in life, half-covered with an American flag and half with a Yugoslavian flag. Unfathomably, his electrically vibrant mind is dead, like an expired battery. The eighty-six-year-old corpse is that of Nikola Tesla, a Serbian immigrant who once stood beside electrical wizards, like Thomas Edison, George Westinghouse, and the younger atomic breed, like Albert Einstein and Enrico Fermi.

As I cough from the musky smell of incense, my somber trance unexpectedly dies as my rookie FBI partner, Billy Davis, slides into the pew next to me. With eyes wide and his youthful face white as the snow outside, he removes his fedora and whispers, "Bad news, sir!"

I blink hard, glancing back at Tesla's coffin. "Worse than *this*?"

Billy swallows hard as he places his fedora on his lap, then begins his nervous tick of spinning his shiny new college ring on his finger. "Yes! Foxworth and thirty-five others are dead! Shot down over the Atlantic."

My adrenaline surges as I stand up, grasp his fidgety hand, and escort him through the throng of two thousand mourners into the antechamber. "What happened, and who's responsible?" I ask in a whisper.

"Not sure," Billy says as he now nervously fumbles with his fedora. "But it must be the damn Krauts. All I know is that they were flying to meet President Roosevelt in Casablanca, when our naval fleet radioed the sighting. Big explosion, *bang!* Gone! Do you think the damn Nazis managed to steal Tesla's Dooms Day plans?"

I shake my head. "You mean his *Death Ray* plans. No, Billy. It's too soon for anyone to develop it that fast. As far as I know, Tesla never got around to finalizing those plans."

The fact is, Tesla's death—five days ago, on January 7, 1943—caused a renewed interest in the neglected wizard. While many felt that Tesla had lost his youthful brilliance to become a deranged dreamer and publicity hound—such as his fantastical claim of a death ray that could eliminate all attacks by air and sea—many others knew the eccentric genius could never be discounted completely.

The FBI investigation of Tesla began surreptitiously about a year ago. Our assistant director, P.E. Foxworth, assigned me, Mario Porcello, to the case and I asked to have young Billy Davis join me. Foxworth had questioned my choice. He expected me to pick a seasoned veteran, but my selection was actually twofold. First, I was looking to pass along some of my hard-learned experience. And second, I was hoping to alleviate the ribbing Billy got from our hardnosed peers. Good intentions aren't always the wisest choices, but noble efforts must be taken, at least once in a while.

Anyhow, I had taken onto this case with real gusto; interviewing Tesla's associates and reading anything I could get my hands on. The things that emanated out of this man's head were akin to those from Leonardo Da Vinci's. Basically, off-the-charts brilliant. And for many years, I've been privy to how J.P. Morgan and other financiers had made some appalling decisions, cutting Tesla's funding and projects that could have reaped incredible rewards if given the chance.

As a kid living in Shoreham, Long Island, back in 1903, I recall vividly the day I saw Tesla's colossal Wardenclyffe tower, which Morgan scantily financed with $150,000. Being a curious tyke, I had wandered through the woods many times to get a closer glimpse of the immense wooden structure, with its octagonal-shaped stem and mushroom-like metallic dome. And I'll never forget the several electrifying nights when Tesla fired it up. Huge blinding bolts of electricity shot upward from its metal dome, igniting the clouds into a massive lightshow of staggering proportions, as if Zeus ignited the aurora borealis.

Having read how the power surge from Tesla's laboratory in Colorado Springs was so immense that it blew out the city's entire electrical grid, I had anticipated a similar fate. Yet while Shoreham was spared, Tesla's project was not. Morgan, Astor, and Westinghouse had terminated funding. As such, Tesla's dreams of transmitting electrical power, radio waves, and visual transmissions were dashed, the tower being dynamited soon after the breakout of war. That order came from the United States government who feared Tesla or others could use it for treasonous communications or its enormous power source as a death ray.

Meanwhile, Tesla's hopes were that his tower would peacefully interconnect the entire world, like a huge brain, allowing everyone to communicate with one another, both verbally and visually. A bizarre claim, indeed, but one never knows what a Leonardo or a Tesla are capable of, as every so often nature breeds a very select few with exceptional ideas, ideas that demand fertilization to grow. But the financial farmers of lesser intelligence often fail to do so, leaving these precious crops to wither and scatter on the winds of time, only to die or take root decades or centuries later.

But when news of Tesla's death hit the papers, my bureau gained access to his apartment in the Hotel New Yorker two days later. Under the bogus directive of the Office of Alien Property, we ransacked his apartment, seizing and impounding all of Tesla's documents and scientific paraphernalia. I say bogus, because Tesla had become a United States citizen many decades ago, yet with the war going on in Europe and the Pacific, ethnic profiling had become an unfortunate necessity. Even Enrico Fermi had faced racial roadblocks for being Italian, which prevented him from working on a top-secret project. But according to one of my sources, FDR pulled some strings and cleared him.

As I stand in the crowded vestibule of the St. John Divine Cathedral, my mind reels. My assistant director and his entire crew are all dead. I was supposed to be on that plane, but the matter of my wife being pregnant literally saved my life. That she's over forty and I'm two years shy of half-a-century only adds to that miracle. How fickle this fragile game of life is.

Shaking these thoughts from my head, I now have to concentrate on who killed my boss and his crew. I look at my twenty-year-old rookie partner, with his blonde curly hair and freckled face, and say, "Perhaps it *was* the Germans, Billy. The Atlantic is a shooting gallery."

Billy nods as more mourners file into the church, either to bid farewell to a national treasure or nosily gape at a curious spectacle.

"It sure is a duck shoot," Billy finally says. "My brother's convoy was hit by a damn wolf pack. One destroyer was torpedoed and sunk." Nervously, he scratches his baby-skinned chin. "We really must get going, sir. The office wants us to report back immediately."

Catching a cab, we barrel through the cold and windy streets of Manhattan in a yellow '41 Packard and arrive at headquarters. As we step in, I see that the office is a mixture of solemn mutes and babbling motor mouths, the latter projecting their emotionally driven theories along with sinister methods of vengeance. Amid this squall, the names of Hitler, Himmler, Goering and other high-ranking Nazis resonate with vindictive fury.

Calmly, I walk into the cacophonic center of the room and clear my throat. All eyes dart my way and mouths cease to articulate. They know *I* am the lead agent now, who knows more about Tesla than anyone else in the bureau. Which isn't a whole lot, since Tesla had become a recluse for many years, locking himself up in his hotel apartment and coming out only to feed the pigeons in Bryant Park or make a bold statement to the press about some new-fangled device he invented.

Having won my coworkers' rapt attention, I peel off my leather gloves and say, "This tragic event was most likely perpetrated by the Germans, but we mustn't rule out the Soviets."

Special agent Hank Wesley shakes his cocky head and snickers. "No way, Porcello. The Russians are our allies. It's your fellow I-talians who are our enemies."

Jim Hadley interjects, "Yeah. Why would the Russians want to shoot down a friendly?"

Ignoring Hank's insult, my eyes glance at Jim, then sweep across the room. I slap my gloves across my other hand. "Because killing Foxworth and our fellow FBI agents *wasn't* the reason. The information they believe our agents had and were about to deliver to President Roosevelt *is* the reason. And that information had to do with Tesla's claim of having invented a death ray."

Hank and Jim burst out laughing as Hank belches, "A death ray? Ha! I think Tesla toyed around with electricity for far too long, Mario, because his brain was fried!" Eliciting a guffaw from the entire staff, the emboldened comedian continues, "That claim of his was pure poppycock, cooed by a bird-brained pigeon feeder."

"Yeah, Tesla was a real quack all right," Jim adds to another round of laughter.

"Listen," I say as I raise my hand in a conceding fashion. "Tesla *did* have some odd quirks, like demanding that his apartment's door number be divisible by three, or having a stack of eighteen napkins at every meal, but he also developed alternating current, which had catapulted our antiquated world into the modern age." As the cackles start to simmer, I shove the gloves into my coat pocket and continue, "Edison's flawed and disastrous direct current had caused numerous fires and deaths, not to mention being woefully inadequate and incapable of handling variable currents. Without Tesla's significant contribution, Edison would never have been able to electrify New York City or the rest of the world."

Amid a room of near silence and baffled faces, Jim says, "That's all well and good, Mario, but I'm hearing rumors that Tesla might have been murdered by a Nazi spy. So this Soviet accusation of yours seems as far fetched as Tesla's claim of a death ray."

"Yeah," Hank adds. "I think you've gotten too close to your subject, Porcello. You're starting to think like that Serbian lunatic."

My teeth grit as I reply, "You're just xenophobic, Hank."

While Hank squints, stuck on the word like a loon in tar, and our fellow agents stand mute like baffled dodo birds, I continue, "Do you all realize that *that* lunatic developed several key patents that Marconi used to develop wireless radio, and countless other patents that are the seeds to even greater inventions not yet discovered." I exhale heavily, while Billy looks up at me like a younger brother—or more aptly, a son—reveling in my mounting rebuttal, as I continue, "I could go on and on, but suffice it to say, Tesla was eighty-six and in very bad health, so I see no reason to believe it was foul play." Confidently, I brush the snowflakes off my overcoat, and continue, "And I think it's foolish to only label the Nazis as the culprits who shot down Foxworth and his crew. Although Tesla's plans for his death ray were probably not finished, I do know that he previously sold portions of his plans to the Russians in nineteen thirty-nine for twenty-five thousand dollars. So I do believe the allure of a death ray is enough to make any of our friends or foes literally *kill* to make sure *we* don't get it first."

As Billy folds his arms and grins with satisfaction, the rest of our cohorts gaze at me with rapt attention.

Commandingly, I conclude, "Uncle Joe may be our ally, but from the reliable sources I've spoken to, Stalin and his commissars are sadistic murderers, just like Hitler and his henchmen. So if the NKGB believes Foxworth had Tesla's plans with him to relay to FDR, then that makes a pretty darn good reason to sink his butt into the Atlantic."

Amid the sea of pensive faces, Assistant Director Harold Reeks finally steps forward, and bellows, "I'm on board with you, Mario. Best we get you and Billy on a plane to Europe ASAP to investigate further."

Billy turns his gaze toward our boss; his youthful face now pale as the snow outside. "Cross the Atlantic! Are you looking to get us both killed, Chief?"

A round of chuckles and snickers breaks out, while some heatedly shake their heads.

It's times like this that make it hard to be anything but blunt, as I say, "Billy, we can't allow our enemy to paralyze us with fear. Now, tuck those chicken feathers in your coat and let's go!"

Inciting a guffaw, I grasp Billy's fedora from his nervous hand, place it squarely on his head, and nudge him toward the exit.

Hopping on a Douglas DC-3, I instruct Billy to never again voice his fears in front of our fellow agents, who have all committed to putting their lives on the line for our country, adding that if he does, *I* will be the first to rib him, again! With a gracious nod, Billy acknowledges my advice, and we buckle up.

Flying a northern course over the Arctic, we land in London for a brief layover, where we are given our Waffen uniforms and false identification papers. We then set sail, arriving in Nazi-occupied Norway by sea.

Having memorized our new identities and already having an adequate command of the German language, Billy and I disembark at the port village of Halhjem, then travel down a series of winding roads, weaving through the beautiful lake-and-river-infested terrain, and arrive in the city of Oslo.

I had opted to target Oslo since I suspected that the Nazis were developing secret weapons somewhere along the

Baltic coast, either in occupied territory in Norway or perhaps in Germany itself. Moreover, being this much closer to Russia, my hopes were to kill two birds with one stone. The Soviets and Nazis were my prime suspects for anyone seeking a super weapon, and Tesla's death ray certainly was an enticing bit of science fiction, which I'm sure many engineers would love to make non-fiction.

Over the ensuing weeks, Billy and I infiltrated the community, subtly extracting information from stationed German officers and Norwegian locals.

It's a Friday night, once again, and we decide to hit a local gin mill to loosen up the tongues of a few Waffen officers we had recently befriended.

As we enter, SS-*Oberführer* Johann Hochstrasser spots me and cries out, "Ah, Manfred, my friend! And your scrawny sidekick, Eckhard. Come join us."

Having grown accustomed to our new Aryan names, Billy, aka Eckhard, and I sit down at Johann's table. Johann's fellow *Oberführer*, Karl, and a Norwegian cobbler, named Torbjørn, accompanies him.

While I sport a similar SS-*Oberführer* rank and uniform as my two fellow German officers, Billy was unhappily saddled with the lower-ranking SS-*Untersturmführer* insignia.

As drinks begin to flow—and our beautiful Norwegian waitress, Alvina, purposely flaunts her cleavage for our pleasure while bending over to serve us—the night is off to a grand start.

Hanging on the weathered, wood-planked walls are a variety of nautical trinkets, including old astrolabes, block and tackle, and even a small replica of a Viking longship, giving our new haunch a real gritty flavor of old-world Norwegian seamanship.

Minutes roll by, turning into hours, as I strategically keep my subjects well lubricated and extract valuable information from them amid this ever-darkening and dingy little pub. Scruffy-looking Norwegian locals, many of whom are weathered fishermen, drink ales and alcohol while smoking stinky cigars that fill the pub with drifting veils of tobacco smoke, making me feel like I'm back on the fog-laden streets of London. Yet the two Nazi storm troopers sitting at the bar obliterate any notion of friendly territory.

Taking a swig of my Linie Aquavit (Norway's aromatic spirit), I return my gaze to our table, only to realize that Johann seems to be on an ornery roll tonight, pumping Billy like a bilge pump. "So, Eckhard, you say you're from Hamburg, yet you don't know the *Gröninger Braukeller*? What kind of German are you?"

Billy's face begins to turn whiter and whiter, as Karl joins in, his demeanor getting sharper, like his Waffen-issued dagger. "*Ja,* how can that be, Eckhard?" Karl says in his thick German accent. "You certainly enjoy your beer."

And at that, Karl was right. I had been concentrating on my three subjects so much that I failed to realize how Billy was getting sloshed, as he nervously rubs his sweaty chin and burps. "W-well, I g-guess I lived on t-the other side of town, b-boys."

Johann and Karl's eyes begin to squint, suspicious, while I discreetly put my hand on my holster, snap it open, and put a tense grip on my Walther P38.

I smile. "My good friends, Eckhard is just a young lad. Cut him some slack. He was never a drinker back home, and only took to the bottle after this crazy war started."

Johann and Karl gaze my way, their cold, piercing eyes seeking to decipher if I'm truly an Aryan or a loathsome Yank.

Thankfully, Torbjørn, whom I've grown to trust, cut in. "Gentlemen, please. Relax!" he says while lighting up a cigarette. "How about another round?"

Torbjørn and I had met several times previously. Although suspicious of me at first, the subjugated cobbler was becoming more receptive to my private declarations of being a good, ethical German with no malice in my heart or sympathy for the Nazi Party. I've come to believe that Torbjørn is just a provincial businessman who would love to see his country free of the Nazis' iron fist and their goose-stepping black-leather boots.

Luckily, Alvina overhears Torbjørn's call for another round and quickly begins replenishing our drinks with a calming smile.

Meanwhile, Billy's eyes are still floating in a sea of suds as he clumsily knocks over his mug.

Karl recoils as the ale rolls across the table and onto his lap. Jumping to his feet, he spits, *"Du dummkopf!"*

Billy lunges to his feet and snaps, "Shut the hell up!" in English.

Before Billy's fist lands on Karl's chin, I had already pulled out my pistol and pointed it a Johann's face. As Karl begins careening backward across the floor, I rise to my feet. "Don't move, Johann!"

Johann's beady eyes glow with venom as he spits, "Manfred, you two-faced bastard!" Filling with rage, he reaches for his Luger.

I fire a shot into his forearm, causing him to nurse his bleeding wound, while I now point my Walther at Karl, who is leaping back up to his feet. "Don't be foolish, Karl! As you can see, I'm not afraid to use this."

Meanwhile, the other patrons are sitting with dropped jaws and their tongues tied in Norwegian knots, dumfounded, while the two storm troopers were fortunately in the John.

No sooner do I ask Alvina to get Johann a towel to stop his bleeding, than he defiantly pulls out his Luger with his bloody hand and points it at me. As I divert my pistol from Karl back to Johann, Johann's bullet bores through my left shoulder. Gritting my teeth, I take aim, and blow a hole in Johann's chest, knocking him backward to the floor.

Meanwhile, Karl had pulled out his pistol, pointed it at Billy, and with a grunt, now pulls the trigger. His Luger jams! As Karl begins to re-cock it, I take aim and unload a chunk of lead into his neck. But before Karl keels over, he unloads a second shot! To my horror, Billy falls fatally to the floor—his youthful body by my feet with a bullet lodged deep in his skull.

As the two storm troopers emerge from the restroom with guns drawn, Torbjørn grabs my hand firmly and quickly begins ushering me out the rear door with a cloth and bottle of booze in his other hand. Into the dark night we run as bullets whiz precariously over our heads.

Two weeks have gone by since Torbjørn cleaned my wound with brandy and stitched me up, as if one of his customers' torn leather shoes. Fortunately, the bullet had gone straight through me, but the loss of my young buddy, Billy, had also gone straight through me, like a bulldozer. I was crushed. Losing a partner is like losing a brother. But in Billy's case, it was like losing a son. For days I mourned, as thoughts of his innocent young face flashed in my mind. His nervous tick of twisting his college ring or his puppy dog smile was sorely missed, and now cherished. Fortunately, we at least managed to retrieve his body, which is set to ship home.

The good news, however, is that, Torbjørn and his friends were in the resistance and divulged a wealth of valuable intelligence, including their covert Operation Gunnerside to sabotage Vemork, the German's nuclear weapons plant some three hours west of Oslo. However, the biggest windfall was that before I killed Johann I had managed to extract from him where the Nazis' secret rocket factory was located. As I suspected, it was on the northern coast of Germany, in the little village of Peenemünde.

Having relayed that critical intelligence back to headquarters, Operation Hydra commenced several months later in August of 1943, being the first air raid to disrupt Nazi Germany's development of V1 and V2 rockets. Some 600 Avro Lancaster bombers struck Peenemünde at midnight, causing massive destruction to the weapons factories and killing almost 800 workers. Other missions followed and eventually, over a year later, the free world celebrated VE Day on May 8, 1945.

And while I never solved the mystery of who shot down my assistant director over the Atlantic, I did learn just recently, some forty-years later, that the Soviets *are* attempting to build some type of doomsday weapon. So my hunch appears to have been correct.

However, President Reagan is convinced that the Soviets will fail, due to their aberrant ideology and broken economy, and is brazenly countering with his fantastical Star Wars initiative, a program that most assuredly is gleaning ideas from Tesla's death ray schematics, just as the Soviets probably are. So Tesla's dream—which was not an offensive death ray, but rather a defensive device to render an opponent's weaponry useless and thus end war—might very well come to fruition.

For, as I said, it is a sad fact of human nature that the clairvoyant visions of geniuses (like Nikola and Leonardo) often die—or materialize decades or centuries later—due primarily to the neglect or stupidity of their so-called "superior" patrons.

Fortunately, these days I've long been retired and can focus on positive matters, since on my return home from Norway, back in 1943, my pregnant wife had given birth to twin girls. We had named them Nicola and Leonora.

Hey, one never knows.

Tito's Tortured Mind

My eyes rolled out of the darkness and into the bizarre vision before me. A congregation of wild-eyed monkeys surrounded me; each holding Y-shaped sticks, as if pitchforks. It was then that I noticed my hands and feet were tied. Long sinewy vines wrapped around my wrists and ankles secured me to a stump. Glancing around, I realized I was seated in the middle of a strange and foreboding forest. Gnarled plant life merged with the gloomy gray sky into a swirling soup of dreary illusion, making for a surreal backdrop to the insanity before me.

Emerging out of the mist, a large monkey swaggered through the apish throng. As his cohorts began chanting, the alpha monkey turned and gazed deep into my eyes. A chill rippled my skin as his evil eyes stayed fixed on me, glowing with ominous intent. Then, unexpectedly, the hairy ape raised the hand he had concealed behind his back. My eyes froze! Clutched in his strong, leathery hand was a sharpened piece of slate. There was no mistaking it—this ape had crafted a sharp Chai Dao knife.

My heart raced as he stepped toward me. Perspiration ran down my face, along the crest of my jaw and down my pulsating neck. Fixing me with his wild-eyed gaze, the alpha ape snorted, then growled, igniting a frenzy of jarring screams as his cohorts jumped and thrust their crude wooden pitchforks into the air like savage warriors.

With a lightning-fast swipe, the ape's arm swept across my forehead, the razor-sharp slate slicing the top of my skull off in one fell swoop! Numb with shock, I was stupefied. Yet the horror had only just begun. With my brain exposed and wriggling from the trauma, the monkeys dived into the cranial feast, scooping and devouring my panic-stricken tissue and thoughts.

I bolted upright in bed! My eyes blazed open to see the glimmer of dawn as the musty smell of my army barracks reaffirmed my return to reality. Soaked with sweat, I sighed, as Lieutenant Freddy "Hotfoot" Fallon kicked my bunk. "Tito… I mean Colonel Romano. Get up! We take off in fifteen minutes."

My dazed eyes blinked hard, then glanced down at my lap. Sitting on top of my blanket was my book, entitled *Casual Chat on Mantuolou's Veranda,* written by Zhang HaiOu in the mid-19th century. A smile of relief etched my weary face. Zhang's journal had told of a bizarre delicacy in China—*monkey brains.* He described how they tied a monkey underneath a round table with only the top of its sliced-off head sticking up in the middle so dining guests could eat its brains while it was still alive. I shook my head. "Jesus Christ!" I mumbled. "*Humans* are brutal animals."

Captain Charlie Amato didn't hear me as he zipped up his flight suit and looked my way. "Colonel. You look like hell. What gives?" He leaned toward me and whispered with a giggle, "Did you have another love dream about Anna and soil your boxers?"

I smirked. "No, Captain Chuckles," I whispered back, being very familiar with Charlie Amato's railleries. "And that's no way to talk to your commanding officer."

"Well, Colonel," he replied, as he stood erect and spoke openly, "After today's sortie you'll be a free man, you lucky son of a gun. So all I'm saying is, I guess you can't wait to run home to Anna, right?"

Not wishing to reveal my personal heartache to my men I remained silent, while Freddy did one of his typical hotfoot moves. Comically, he danced with himself, then spun around. With his back facing us, his head moved as if kissing a dame, while his hands massaged his back. "Oh, Anna, I miss you so so much!" he said to a barrage of laughter.

I rolled my eyes as Navigator Johnny Landon took a drag of his Lucky Strike and belched with a giggle. "With all due respect, Lieutenant Fallon, you're a blockhead!"

Meanwhile, bombardier Eddy Hansen quipped, "Yeah, that's the only dame you could ever get, Hotfoot."

Charlie laughed. "But by the looks of those man hands on that broad I think you're sucking face with a drag queen."

I shook my head. "All right, that's enough, you slaphappy bunch of stooges." Eliciting another round of laughter, I continued, "Yes, this *is* my last mission. But remember, I *did* fly eight more sorties than the required thirty just to be with you boys." As they simmered to my serious tone, I added, "And, yes, I can't wait to get back to the States. But every sortie we fly is a dangerous one, so don't let your guard down for my sake."

Charlie smirked. "Colonel, our limey friends here have been good hosts, but I wish I was joining you. I'm ready to leave their pompous King and Queen to return home to our down-to-earth republic. You know, the one that kicked their imperialistic asses off our continent."

As a few airmen laughed and others shook their heads, I retorted, "Captain Amato! I told you before; I don't appreciate that kind of talk." As I zipped up my leather A-2 jacket over my electric-heated suit, I added, "So if that pisses you off, do it in the latrine."

Charlie smirked as Freddy chimed in, "Colonel, I have nothing against the Brits. In fact, I think they're rather swell, especially the ones with skirts. But you gotta admit, them taking the easy flights at night, while we get stuck fighting the Krauts in broad daylight, ain't no way to make friends."

"Look, men," I said to all. "Ike managed to become Supreme Allied Commander, surpassing generals here who had better credentials. So we've been damn lucky to be their guests and to finagle that *supreme* position. So, in my book, I think we got the upper hand. Furthermore, although it looks like we'll certainly win this war, England will surely be one of the losers. There's no way, between their debt and how FDR and Stalin will divvy up the world in the aftermath, that Churchill could possibly hold onto all their colonies. So after all this hard fighting England *will* lose their empire."

Johnny Landon shook his head. "Yeah, I get that, Colonel, but it's still not fair. Flying during the day has been one helluva grind." His eyes glazed up. "Benny was a great buddy and only seventeen. He was a darn good navigator. I enjoyed mentoring that little guy until… well, until…" Johnny choked up and pinched his eyes closed, sequestering the tear. After a brief moment he reopened them. "And it's not just Benny, Colonel. Christ, how many others did we lose? Eighty? A hundred? I lost count."

"Okay, enough, Johnny," I said, dispensing with military formality, as I always did when emotions ran high.

"We all lost friends. Damn good boys, all of them. But so too did the Brits. It's war; dirty, rotten, bloody war, and I can't have any bellyaching. Put it behind you. We can't change the past, but we *can* have a say about our future. The more Jerries we shoot down the closer we'll be to winning this damn war. And the closer you'll all be to going home, like me."

Charlie clutched his helmet and goggles. "That's right, boys, and who are we to bellyache when the colonel stuck with us more than he had to?" He swiveled toward me. "I apologize for starting this crummy ball rolling, Colonel." He gazed at the crew and stomped his foot. "All right, boys!" he barked. "It's time to kick some Krauts out of the sky. Buckle up and lets fly!"

As we exited our barrack, the frigid November air chilled our faces, while a sturdy wind blew. It was 1944 and Allied Forces were eager to end the war, which seemed closer than ever before. As we all walked onto the tarmac toward our enormous B-24 Liberator, Johnny shook his head. "There's our big, bulky aluminum box. That ugly bird could probably house a B-17 in it."

Freddy shot Johnny a mocking glare. "Hey, chowder head, that ugly duckling has bombed the crap out of a lot of Nazis. I love that aluminum hulk."

Charlie looked my way as he slipped on his gloves. "Colonel, with this being your last flight and all, I think you should fly a B-17 today."

Johnny nodded. "He's right, Colonel, you must. That bird can hit 29,000 feet. Leave the nitty-gritty low-level bombing to us in the B-24 Titanic."

I shook my head. "No way, boys. And our trusty *Big Bird* is no *Titanic,* Johnny."

Charlie grasped my arm. "Colonel, we insist! There's no need for you to take an unnecessary risk today, of all days. Think of Anna. Think of home. Or just think of this request as our way of saying thanks."

As the rest of the crew chimed in, I smiled while my hand discreetly rubbed my pocket, feeling my once cherished photo of Anna. It's not easy concealing pain, but the war certainly helped in hardening a guy to deal with internal woes. "Very well," I said. "Captain Amato, you can pilot *Big Bird* with our crew. Freddy, you'll be copilot. I'll make arrangements to fly Colonel Patterson's B-17. I think the old crow is due for a rest in the nest anyhow."

As the men chuckled, bombardier Eddy Hansen veered toward me. "Colonel, permission to go with you, sir?" he pleaded, as the warm vapor from his mouth wafted in the cold breeze.

As others likewise asked to join me, I shook my head. "No! I want you all together. You're like a fist. Take some fingers away and you lose your punch. But I appreciate the gesture. I truly do."

Eddy gazed at me with his sly, humorous smile. "No offense, Colonel, but it's not *you* I care about. It's just that I never got to drop bombs from a B-17 at those high altitudes."

As the boys all laughed, I smiled. "Okay, Eddy. Your warm and fuzzy sentiment is duly noted. I'll drag you along." Then before the others could make similar pleas, I barked, "And *only* Eddy! Now get ready for take off."

While the crew did their pre-flight checks, and Eddy waited on the tarmac, I checked in at HQ to acquire clearance to sub for Colonel Patterson. With everything set, I dug into my pocket and pulled out my photo of Anna. I gazed at it affectionately. Then as I exited, I crunched it into a ball and tossed the painful memory into a trashcan.

Reconnecting with Eddy, who was impatiently slapping his thighs to the beat of Glenn Miller's *In the Mood,* we then climbed into our sleek new bird and met our crew. As we took our places, the B-17 bomber felt a bit cramped, at least compared to our B-24 *Big Bird.*

Eddy balked that the B-17 only had two racks holding twelve bombs. But his eyes lit up when he spotted the Sperry ball turret with its dual .50 caliber machine-guns. Located on the underbelly of the fuselage, the ball turret was currently retracted, sitting inside the fuselage. A scrawny teenaged gunner opened the hatch, winked at Eddy, then squeezed inside the cramped ball of glass and metal.

I put my crush cap on. "Okay, Eddy. Never mind the Flash Gordon technology. Get into position and ready yourself for take off."

"Yes, sir!" Eddy barked.

Meanwhile, I took my seat in the cockpit. Greeting my copilot, Paul, and navigator, Frank, I then gazed out the window at my crew in the B-24. Charlie peered over through his side window and gave me a thumbs up! I returned the gesture and our squadron began taxiing along the runway. Charlie positioned *Big Bird,* and then hit the throttle. The 70,000-pound hunk of aluminum picked up speed slowly, as its four 14-cylinder Pratt & Whitney engines roared. I held my breath, knowing that the hefty B-24 always needed more runway than allotted. As expected, Charlie chewed up several yards of grass after the runway to get off the ground.

I sighed with relief.

I opened my personal journal and scribbled *Thursday, November 2, 1944. Ready to take off from RAF Andover airbase. Crew in B-24. Eddy & I in B-17. Target: Leipzig. My last mission! Godspeed to us all.*

I was about to add *I'm crushed, like the photo of Anna. Yet I understand a woman can't wait forever.* But I closed the journal instead. There was no need to write what I knew in my broken heart or to tell my crew. It was my heartache, one I'd just have to bury, like all the deaths of my buddies. As I've said to myself many times: Purge the pain and try to find a glimmer of hope to light a path forward. It was crucial to keep my brain uncluttered and healthy, yet that was another battle, even tougher than all of our dangerous missions.

I turned and yelled to the crew. "Are all your rheostats and oxygen masks operational? And don't forget your gloves. It's going to get damn cold up there."

With temperatures dropping to forty to sixty degrees below zero at high altitude it was crucial to have heated suits and three layers of gloves. Tommy Benson had to have his fingers amputated due to frostbite. He had taken off his gloves to fix a jammed machine-gun; those thirty seconds cost him eight fingers.

As the crew all bellowed, "Check!" I pushed the throttle forward. The B-17 took off like a graceful eagle into the frigid blue sky. As we climbed to 10,000 feet, I double-checked that everyone had their oxygen masks on. We then climbed to 20,000 feet and hovered about a hundred feet above my crew in the *Big Bird,* despite pleas from my new copilot and navigator to climb higher for safety reasons.

I had to keep a close eye on my boys, and being that these B-17 fellows always flew near the rim of the stratosphere, in the *safer zone,* I could understand Paul and Frank's concerns. But all my B-24 missions had been in the tumultuous troposphere, so I knew I could get us through this in one piece.

Holding my course, we eventually approached Leipzig. Within minutes, the familiar yet always frightening bursts of flak exploded all around us. Huge billows of black smoke passed by our windshield as we cruised through a vaporous sea of dark death. Sunlight flickered, as the flak became more frequent and violent.

Frank stared at his cathode ray tube, and called out, "I'm getting a lot of grass, Colonel! Those damn Krauts are jamming my Gee Box with spurious radio signals." As his face glowed green from the phosphor in his radar screen, he added, "But I managed to get a good reading. Ready yourselves, boys, we're approaching the IP."

With the initial point of releasing our bombs upon us, I banked to get a better look at my squadron below. I radioed to Charlie, "Let's do this and go home!"

I could see Charlie through his window look my way. With a nod, he radioed, "Yes, sir. But you had better climb out of here, *fast,* Colonel! The flack is getting more intense."

"Never mind me, Captain. Do your job. Destroy the oil refinery. Now!"

With a thumbs up, I saw Charlie nod, while Freddy leaned over and echoed the gesture. The B-24's bomb bay doors opened and a flurry of bombs began dropping from its belly, looking like a huge silver shark laying a barrage of deadly eggs.

From behind me, Eddy barked, "Bombs away!" as our own load began to rain down.

Just then a team of Focke-Wulf 190 D-12s came screaming up through the clouds. The fast and furious Nazi fighters, with their BMW 801 radial engines, split up and began attacking in all directions. Like a swarm of killer wasps, they fired their MK 108 30 mm cannons through their propellers, stinging the bellies of several B-24s below us.

Frank, once again, prodded, "Colonel Romano, I suggest that we climb to 28,000 feet ASAP! The FWs can't climb that high."

Before I could answer, I heard a tremendous explosion. Quickly, I turned to look out the window. *Big Bird* was hit! The entire right wing had been sheered off, as fire and smoke streamed in its wake. My heart dropped and eyes bulged, as I radioed, "Charlie! Get the boys suited up and *jump!* NOW!"

Charlie and Freddy glanced over, fear marred their faces, as the plane began to list and pull away. A dreadful lump welled in my throat as adrenaline surged through my veins. In utter horror, I watched as their cockpit ignited on fire. Charlie and Freddy tried beating back the flames with their jackets, but the inferno grew with such ferocity that they had to submit to their fate. A chill went through my body as they turned to face me. As fire raged around them, Freddy ignited like a gasoline-soaked rag, while Charlie gazed at me, his eyes piercing into my soul with a gut-wrenching look of resignation. Bravely, he saluted farewell.

Tears filled my eyes. It was the most painful salute I ever had to return. Helpless, I watched my beloved crew slip further away as the B-24 spiraled down in flames.

Dear God! My mind raced, *I was supposed to be on that plane with them.* My jaw clenched tight and nostrils flared as I barked, "We're going down!"

Paul's head snapped in my direction. "Are you nuts!? We must go *up*. We can finish our mission at 28,000 feet."

Frank glanced up from his radar screen and pleaded the same, while Eddy Hansen climbed forward and tapped my shoulder. "Colonel, take us *down!* We can't let those filthy Krauts get away with that."

I turned to catch Eddy's eyes. "How many more bombs do we have left?"

"Three, sir."

I paused to listen to my headset, then looked at my copilot. "This is not just personal anymore, Paul. The rest of our squadron just radioed in. They only hit secondary targets. They *missed* the oil refinery. Accuracy, as you know, is greatly diminished at 28,000 feet. So we are going down!" My eyes glanced at Frank. "Understood?"

"Y-yes, Colonel," he stuttered. "Understood. I'll make the calculations."

Gazing back at Eddy, I added. "Get those 500 pound babies ready. We have a special delivery to make."

"Yes, sir!" Eddy barked with a passionate salute.

As I passed the command along to the rest of the crew, our gunners swiveled into place. Down below us, our fellow bombers split up. Those with empty bomb bays headed home, while the others unleashed their M2 Browning machine-guns, firing at the German fighters.

As Frank issued coordinates, I steered the B-17 down through the deadly web of dogfights toward our target.

Meanwhile, Eddy brazenly straddled himself over the open bomb-bay doors, and clutched onto a steel railing. With the wind blowing through his hair, he said, "I can see the oil refinery. When the hell am I gonna get the order, Frank? It looks like we might miss the MPI!"

I glanced over at our navigator. "Frank! Let's go! We can't miss the Mean Point of Impact."

Frank's face flushed. "Colonel, I'm n-not familiar with calculating targets at this low altitude. You've taken us d-down to 5,000 feet. This is i-insane, sir!"

"Shit!" I spat, as I swung my head toward the rear. "Eddy, use your best judgment, we only get one shot at this."

As Eddy acknowledged my command, an FW 190 came screaming into view.

"Jerry at three o'clock!" Paul yelled with bulging eyes.

Our gunners swung their guns down toward the oncoming target and opened fire.

From behind me, Eddy bellowed, "Bombs away!"

As we flew past the refinery, our young turret gunner cheered, "Whoa! I nailed the Fat Wanker!"

Banking to the right, I gazed out the windshield to get a glimpse of the kill. As sure as sarsaparilla, the FW fighter was on fire and careening toward the ground.

"Good job, son!" I said with a chuckle, appreciating his Wanker gibe.

I circled around to get a visual of our main target. As I did, an enormous black cloud of burning petroleum had already engulfed the sky.

Eddy stepped up behind me as we blazed right through it. "Yahoo! We're smoking now, Colonel. What a beautiful sight!"

I smiled. "And what beautiful aim, Eddy. Great job!"

As Paul and Frank each congratulated Eddy, I noticed out of the corner of my eye another FW fighter. This one screaming right toward us!

"Stations, men!" I commanded. "This little dance is *not* over."

Frank clutched his seat and closed his eyes.

Meanwhile our nose gunner unleashed two rounds, when his gun jammed. The Nazi's guns belched fire, spitting a barrage of bullets right at us. Our windshield burst, as slugs riddled the cockpit. Paul screamed as the huge caliber bullet blew a gaping hole in his chest, soared through his seat, and hit Frank square in the face. Frank's eyes had still been closed, so he literally didn't see it coming, yet his entire head exploded, as his decapitated body eerily remained strapped to the seat.

A horrible chill ran through me as I wiped their blood off my face. With my two right-hand men dead, and air blustering through the cockpit, I turned and barked, "Parachutes on!"

As I fought to control the ailerons and rudder, I spotted an open field in the distance, partially blanketed with snow. Both port engines had been strafed and were on fire. I cut back the speed and descended to 4,000 feet, then gave the order, "Abandon ship!"

The crew began bailing out, while Eddy pushed his way forward against the airstream. "Where's your parachute, Colonel?"

I glanced back. "I intend to land in that field, Eddy. But this plane might very well explode on impact. It's best if you all jump now while you can."

"Permission to stay on board, Colonel?"

"Request denied! You're a damn good bombardier, Eddy. When you land, try to locate the resistance and get back to England. Is that understood?"

Eddy's head dropped. "Yes, sir," he uttered as he fastened his parachute. "If we don't meet up, Colonel, I just want you to know… it's been an honor serving you."

I turned and gazed deep into his eyes. "The honor was all mine, Eddy. Now get going. I can't afford to lose—" I choked up, "anymore of you. Godspeed!"

Eddy nodded with a sniffle and saluted.

No sooner did I return the salute than Eddy turned and exited the plane.

Glancing at my two dead comrades beside me, my mind raced. *Was I wrong to ignore their plea to climb away from this hell? Would that have truly ensured our safety? But what about our main target, the refinery? The mission would have been a failure.* I blinked hard. *Jesus Christ! Is* this *success?*

As I looked at their two mutilated bodies, horrifying visions of Charlie and Freddy burning in the cockpit rattled me nauseous. *Good God!* my mind cried. *Why wasn't I with them?* Then I thought of Charlie's last words, "Think of this request as our way of saying thanks." I looked up. *Oh Lord, is that how you had my men thank me? Shit!* I shook my head to expunge the nightmare, then refocused my attention to the grave situation at hand.

The B-17 hummed and moaned as it flew over a thick row of trees. Suddenly, the grassy field appeared. I struggled to keep the plane from listing, while the two dead engines continued to burn. I came down hard and fast, the wheels hitting the icy grass and carving grooves across the field. The tires blew out, and the landing gear gouged deep ravines into the frozen dirt before breaking off. Meanwhile, my eyes widened to the rapidly approaching trees up ahead. Unbuckling myself, I dashed to the rear of the plane and grabbed a structural rib just as the B-17 crashed into the wall of trees. The entire nose of the plane crushed like a beer can.

Tossed to the floor, I then sprang to my feet and clipped on a holster, packed with a Colt. I crept toward the open hatch and gazed out, wondering if my remaining crew managed to find refuge. Beyond the distant, snow-covered trees on the horizon, huge fireballs and thick black smoke despoiled the once blue sky. I smiled. Our handiwork would indeed set the Nazis back several weeks or more.

I jumped out and ran toward the dirt road, some three hundred yards away. Having reached the rutted path, I looked both ways, and listened. What I heard was *not* what I wanted to hear! Quickly, I jumped back into the frosty bushes as a procession of German military vehicles rumbled by. Cascading before me was the menacing vision of Nazi soldiers dressed in their dreary grey uniforms driving their dreary gray vehicles with their Black Death crosses painted on the sides.

Sinking back into the bushes, I had no choice but to wait it out and hope for the best. But the procession suddenly came to a stop. About fifty soldiers hopped out of their vehicles and dashed toward my burning B-17. As I observed them through a thick mesh of snow-covered branches, I crossed myself. *Please God, make this pass.*

My prayers were either too late or not heard, because I suddenly felt the barrel of a rifle lodged in the pit of my back. The crouching Nazi behind me barked, *"Nicht bewegen!"* (Don't move!)

Slowly, I raised my hands, as several Krauts pushed their way through the brush, bayonets pointed at my face.

"The gigi is up!" one said in broken English, as he added, "That *is* how you Yanks say it, *ja*?"

"No! It's *gig*," I retorted. "Perhaps you picked up that French dialect after you broke your treaty and subjugated France."

Scharführer Höfler laughed as he stepped closer and stuffed his Walther P38 back into his holster. "Yes, the French were softer than a crêpe Suzette. Even the dumb Polacks had put up a better fight. But they all eventually fell to our superior forces."

I chuckled.

Höfler squinted. "Is what I say humorous, Colonel?" he demanded, irritated.

"Actually, it is," I said. "Quite comical, in fact. Especially considering that we kicked you out of Northern Africa, swept through Italy, and the Soviets are giving you hell on the Eastern front."

Höfler's lips twisted. "Since you will now be a confined and useless prisoner, I can tell you *this*. We have developed new weapons that will annihilate whole cities. Beyond the V1 buzz bombs, von Braun has finally perfected, and is now launching, his fantastical V2 rockets. London *will* fall, just like Paris, Warsaw, and all the rest!"

I snickered. "You Nazis still don't get it, do you? Do you really think that after Normandy you have a chance? Patton, Bradley, and Montgomery will continue to sweep through your toxic Reich, which they're crushing like weeds under their boots. You're done for, kaput!"

Höfler's burning bravado simmered into smoldering contempt. Irritated, he placed his hand on his hip. "So, are you suggesting that we simply let you go?"

"Sounds like a good idea to me," I said with a cocky smile. "Perhaps I'll even put in a good word for you when we storm through this frozen cesspool."

Höfler gritted his teeth, then belched, "Take this prisoner to the train depot and ship his wise ass to Auschwitz!"

Two guards grabbed my arms and lifted me up, as Höfler added with venom, "That will teach you just how superior you Americans are. I *will* have the last laugh, Colonel!"

They stuffed me into a freezing freight train with other prisoners like cattle. I peered out the thin slits between the wooden planks to see the frigid scenery of Leipzig slowly fade from sight. The train reeked of animal feces and the civilian prisoners were gaunt and petrified. Ten hours later, I peered out once again to see the icy vista of southern Poland. Evidently, Höfler, the dirty devil, was right. For after I passed through the brick portal of Auschwitz–Birkenau, Lucifer's laugh was definitely on *me*. The insanity I witnessed at Birkenau only compounded the traumatic events of losing my dear friends. My mind was a mess. The sight of thousands of cruelly starved men, women, and children—all with shaven heads and numbers tattooed on their arms—being gassed and then incinerated was beyond human comprehension.

Being an Italian-American, and in good health, I evaded immediate extermination. Instead, I was placed with the crematorium commandos, who were mostly Ukrainian, Slavic, and Polish dregs of society. Joining these ex-cons and derelicts, we had the morbid task of incinerating the cadavers and then tossing their ashes into the icy Vistula River. Our barracks were squalid wooden shacks, infested with lice and bed bugs, and totally incapable of keeping out the bitter winter freeze. Disease, depravity, and death surrounded us—as noxious as the Zyklon-B being used to kill all the innocent prisoners, yet without the fatal end result. Our minds and souls suffocated and slowly withered from the poisonous stench. I couldn't fathom how anyone with a soul could ever emerge from this hellish nightmare mentally or morally unscathed.

The days passed into weeks, as the bitter blizzards of Polish winter rolled in. Having seen the SS guards and their female counterparts merrily hanging Christmas balls on frozen pine trees was enough to make me vomit. There must have been some invisible barrier around the death camp, because God certainly didn't exist here.

On Christmas Eve of 1944, SS guard Helmut Goetz approached me. "Colonel Romano, being that you are an officer, would you care to attend our Christmas Eve party? Mind you, it would only be for an hour, before our commandant and superior officers arrive."

Helmut was actually one of the good bad guys, having been fairly humane in his treatment of prisoners. Whether that was innate or the fact that he understood the Reich was imploding, I'm not sure. But still, I had to ask the obvious. "Does anyone here *really* believe in Christ?"

Helmut smirked. "Colonel, while many of my brothers and sisters have fallen under Hitler's evil spell, I assure you, some of us are God fearing men and women."

I squinted in doubt, then snickered. "I fear even God fears Auschwitz."

Helmut gazed down at the drifts of snow and ice, then peered around the camp. Beyond the snowy rooftops, blackish-gray smoke billowed feverishly from the crematorium's towering chimneys, merging with the dreary gray clouds amid twilight. He whispered, "I agree, Tito. I'm not proud of what I had fallen into, whether by fear of death if I defied the Reich or just lack of a strong Christian will." He glanced around to ensure our privacy, and continued, "But I am willing to change all that to save my soul."

"Just what is it you're saying?" I asked as I rubbed my hands together to keep them warm.

Helmut's wary eyes kept scanning the perimeter as he talked. "I'm saying that I can help you and three others to escape. I can supply all of you with civilian clothes, and can manufacture four sets of identification papers and passports. But only four."

I recoiled. "Helmut, you seem like a nice enough fellow, but I'll have to decline. I'll just wait out my time."

"Wait for what? You could be gassed and incinerated on a moment's notice, on a whim. There is *no* security here, even for those who are not Jews, Poles or Slavs."

"I understand that, but as you know, this war is coming to a close, and much sooner than you think. And although I do like you, Helmut, I must confess, I don't trust you."

Helmut's face contorted with disappointment and frustration, while I added, "But I will accept your kind invitation to your Christmas Eve party."

"Very well, Colonel," Helmut replied. "But do know that I *will* get four prisoners to safety. I *will* cleanse my soul, with or without you."

That evening I arrived at the party. All heads turned my way. I was the only male prisoner, and since Helmut allowed me to wear my A-2 jacket with insignia, that didn't sit well with his fellow pack of Waffen wolves. Standing in the corner by the punch bowl were three Jewish female inmates. Their shaved heads and drab prison clothes made for an appalling sight. Meekly, they glanced my way, then resumed their mute and uncomfortable stances. Meanwhile, *Heffernan* (women guards), sported fancy dresses and flaunted their long beautiful hair, as they took pleasure in openly mocking their degraded female subjects.

Helmut whispered, "Never mind them. I loathe most of them. There are only two or three good ones in the lot." He nudged me toward the female prisoners. "You should talk to Emily Weiss. She is an Austrian Jew, quite smart. She does minor secretarial work in Commandant Baer's office."

"Which one is Emily?"

"The pretty one," Helmut said.

I scanned them again and chuckled. "Pretty? Really?"

Helmut smiled. "You just need to use your imagination, Tito. Visualize hair on their heads."

I squinted, then nodded. "Ah, yes, I see what you mean." The initial shock of bald women did take some getting used to. "But why should I speak to *her?*"

"Because Emily has wisely taken my offer to escape. The other women are too afraid. Like you."

I smirked. "I never said I was afraid, Helmut. It's the issue of *trust* that has me skeptical." I straightened out my jacket and stood erect. "I was born and raised in the Bronx, Helmut, and New Yorkers are savvy and skeptical by nature. We have to be, because the craftiest con men seem to make their fortunes there. And I'm not just talking about street hustlers and thugs. Wall Street houses the greediest and most financially successful crooks in the world. Always did, since the days of the previous Roosevelt who tried to bust up their monopolies."

Helmut nodded. "Yes, I had read about your bullish cowboy leader. Teddy seemed like a ball of fire, Tito. But you appear to be a man of such bravado yourself. So, once again, please reconsider my offer." Helmut gently nudged me toward Emily. "At least talk to her."

I glanced at Helmut and rolled my eyes. I then strut through the hostile throng of healthy Nazi predators toward their frail and half-starved prey. As I approached the three pallid women in their drab, gray-striped prison uniforms, they sheepishly moved aside, save for Emily, who stood fixed by the punch bowl. "Can I get you a drink, Colonel?"

As the two other women glanced at me, then shyly at each other, I looked at Emily. Up close her face was indeed beautiful, if you ignored the creases of anguish. "No thank you," I said, as I briefly scanned the room. "I'm not in a festive mood. But I appreciate the offer, Emily."

Her eyes squinted. "How did you know—" she paused, then continued, "Ah, yes of course," she whispered. "Helmut spoke to you. Are you coming?"

I stepped closer, and whispered, "How can you trust him?"

She took a sip of punch, then replied, "Does it matter? I've been here for almost four years. You may have seen a good deal of horror, Colonel, but I assure you, you don't know one tenth of what goes on here."

My face twisted in confusion. "I'm sure I don't. But how did you know I wasn't here long?"

She looked deep into my eyes. "Because you have all your hair. Hair is just one of the many commodities the Nazis reap from prisoners, which they use to stuff their mattresses and pillows for the Reich. And since you still have yours, you must not be Jewish. Nor Polish, Ukrainian, or any other nationality they despise."

"That may explain my being an American, but not how long I've been here."

She smiled. "Well, news of someone as virile and handsome as you would have reached our ears long ago if you *were* here longer."

As I blushed, she added, "And it's splendid to see a *real* man with hair on his head, rather than all these Aryan animals."

I smiled. "Thank you. And I wish I could give you mine. It must be humiliating to be tormented like this."

"We've gotten past that long ago. When one's whole life is stripped of every dignity, with even our names replaced by numbers, one tends to either wither and submit to doom or cling onto hope." She lowered her voice. "I have helped two men escape over the years. Being in a relatively comfortable position in Commandant Baer's office, I felt it was my duty to aid whomever I could to escape, or at least mitigate their torture. But four years of hoping that Allied

Forces will liberate us is enough. It is now *my* turn to escape. And if Helmut is a liar and it fails, who cares at this point. This is no way to live the rest of my life."

I nodded. "I can certainly understand that, Emily. But being a colonel in the United States Air Corps, I know for sure that Hitler's days are numbered. So, I'm going to wait it out. And I hope you will, too."

"That won't happen, Colonel. As I've said," she whispered, "this place is a death factory, and I can't take it anymore." Discreetly, she pointed to a stout woman with long blond hair and a stern, evil expression. "That's Irma Grese, our *rapportführerin.* She takes pleasure in tormenting and torturing women prisoners. While she beats some with her riding crop, others she shoots in cold blood or sends to the gas chamber for no apparent reason. And I wouldn't be surprised if she resorted to the barbaric practice of skinning human cadavers, like Ilse Koch, and using their flesh to make lampshades."

My face contorted with disgust and disbelief, as she continued, "But Irma is a conceited floozy. Against regulations she wears lipstick and eyeliner, and even had an abortion after a fling with Dr. Josef Mengele. He's the Reich's supreme mad scientist, which is a whole other savage story. But on a personal level, Irma Grese appears to have a growing distaste for *me,* apparently not appreciating my close position to the commandant, or perhaps envious of my looks, at least according to my fellow inmates. You see, Irma's jealousy unleashes the Rottweiler in her. So I believe my days are numbered here if I stay."

Feeling numb, I decided to have a glass of punch to wash down the insanity, as Emily continued, "But, as you know, this place is a living nightmare. And if you escape with us, perhaps with your rank and clout you could get the Allies mobilized to liberate this godforsaken madhouse."

Having listened to Emily's logical reasons for over twenty minutes, I finally agreed to join their effort to escape. No sooner did we wrap up our conversation than we were ordered to return to our barracks. Our brief party was over, while the Nazi guards readied themselves for a long evening of liquor, lust, and carefree bouts of laughter.

As planned and promised; Helmut supplied us with civilian clothing and documents. A week later, on New Years Eve, we put our plans into action. Everything had started out like clockwork, yet it didn't take long before one wrench after another jammed up the machine. To my surprise, my suspicion of Helmut attempting to entrap us was ill founded. On the contrary, our mission failed due to our own missteps and unforeseen events. During the escape two of our male compatriots were shot dead, while Emily was dragged back to the women's camp for punishment.

Meanwhile, I was sentenced to three weeks in the cooler, freezing in a small cubical without much food or even the comfort of daylight. In a fit of frustration and self-loathing I bloodied my knuckles by punching the cramped cell walls. It seemed all my earlier successes had crumbled into a string of bloody failures. Enshrouded in darkness, with only my thoughts, my mind traveled to dark places I didn't even know existed. I pondered how one seemingly simple decision could have such devastating consequences. Bad enough we were forced to fend off bullets, bombs, and soulless savages who used poison gas and incinerators to exterminate innocent civilians, but we also had to battle the cerebral war of depression, with its diabolical hallucinations that were so vivid and terrifying that they mauled the mind and bludgeoned the body. It was frightening how fast the human mind creates its own prison amid total darkness. Visions of death are seared into one's brain, as if irrevocable tattoos. Except these images are like 8mm films, the jarring and grainy scenes play over and over again, tormenting the mind and gnawing at the soul, until even your physical frame submits to decay.

The days dragged on and the weeks rolled by as thoughts of my own death became welcome visitors. My spirits were somewhat lifted, however, when the day of my release finally arrived and sunlight washed into my dark little cell. Covered in feces and urine, I slowly exited my dank little pit as my legs struggled to support me. Although the cold fresh air felt good in my lungs and I relished the sight and warmth of the sorely missed sun, I had lost faith that God or life offered anything worth living for. Gazing up at the huge chimneys, still feverishly billowing human ash into the frigid sky, my head dropped. It was useless.

But life throws us curveballs, as two providential occurrences materialized only three days later. It was January 27, 1945. Oddly enough, our long-awaited liberation from Hell didn't come from Heaven above, but rather from Soviet ground troops of the Red Army's 322nd Rifle Division. Despite their often-crude and vengeful ways, the sight of salvation was euphoric, at least for us. German soldiers had previously fled like rats after attempting to kill as many prisoners as possible and destroying evidence that documented their savagery.

Meanwhile, Soviet troops entered the camp to see a jarring sight. Those of us that did survive released sighs; the most profound and poignant sighs to ever waft above a graveyard, for Auschwitz had become the nadir of human hatred and utter depravity. Among the skeletal walking-corpses and human-fueled furnaces that our Soviet liberators found were 370,000 men's suits, 837,000 women's garments, and 8.5 tons of human hair.

The second providential event occurred during the mayhem of liberation, when I ran desperately to find Emily. Having learned that she had been taken to Dr. Mengele's research laboratory, my adrenaline surged, reawakening my thirst for life. Bursting into the facility, I came face-to-face with Mengele's primordial associate, Dr. Werner Metzger. With his crooked teeth, sparse greasy hair, thick round spectacles, and low-sloping forehead that sat atop a bony body, Werner looked more like one of the deformed specimens he was sworn to experiment on or exterminate than the flawless Aryan scientist he was purported to be.

Dr. Mengele had fled earlier, yet Metzger remained, hovering over Emily, hunchbacked and hellbent on completing his radical experiment. Her feet were fastened in stirrups, as if giving birth, and Dr. Metzger was preparing to extract her ovaries to insert them into a female chimpanzee. His mission to discover if Darwin's theory of evolution could be replicated in the matter of months had gripped him so tightly that even Stalin's advancing armies could not deter him. But one soldier did, as I grabbed a chrome vaginal speculum off the instrument table and bashed Metzger in the face, cutting a deep bloody ravine into his left cheek. Werner screamed and dropped his scalpel, as he then feverishly tried to suppress the bloody breach. I unshackled Emily, and together we fled with the liberated masses, happy to have left Dr. Frankenstein and Hades behind.

During our two-week journey through war-torn Europe, Emily and I had apparently fallen prey to our biological instincts. Admittedly, at first I had second thoughts; between suffering through hell on earth together and my rebounding from Anna, I thought it might have been an impulsive whim. But having gazed into Emily's beautiful eyes, and having spent lovely evenings laughing and broaching the mysteries of the universe together, I knew it was not simply a primordial impulse. And that Emily's radiant reddish-brown hair had grown in, framing her adorable face, didn't hurt matters either. As such, we decided to get married once we returned to the States.

On February 14, Valentine's Day, we flew into Idlewild Airport. I secured an apartment at 2486 Hughes Avenue in the Bronx from a humble yet phenomenal man named Michele, an Italian orphan who immigrated to America at age seventeen. Working as a street sweeper and hot dog merchant, Michele managed to save money and buy the apartment building, thus exemplifying the American Dream we had fought Hitler so hard to preserve.

Then came the dreaded moment; the day I introduced Emily to my family. As devout Catholics, my parents were taken aback that my fiancée was Jewish, not to mention our need to live in sin until our wedding day. But they soon warmed to the news that Emily would convert. After Hitler's Final Solution, Emily felt that her chosen status as a Jew presented more disturbing questions than peace and contentment. We married on March 9, 1945 at Our Lady of Mount Carmel Church on 187th Street.

The sacred union and festive reception afterward were grand. Yet dark demons lurked in the shadows. Over the next several months, recurring nightmares from the cooler in Auschwitz returned with a vengeance as battle fatigue gripped my mind and soul. Visions of my buddies burning in their cockpit and saluting farewell seared my mind, as if a red-hot branding iron. The blistering nightmares mushroomed, like the fiery clouds of the bombs we dropped, and grew more intense and more frequent. Disturbing flashes of the stacked corpses of emaciated prisoners being shoveled into furnaces rematerialized, along with the horrid stench, each permeating my crippled senses. I was a mental and physical train wreck.

Emily assertively made inquiries and decided to take me to Allan's Veterans Affairs Hospital. After a brief consultation, they ushered me to a room for observation. My dear wife stayed by my side for six hours until the nurse asked her to leave, instructing her to return the next day. No sooner did Emily leave, than an orderly entered my room with a gurney. As he strapped me in, he assured me it was standard procedure to ensure I didn't have convulsions. He then injected me with a mild sedative to ease my mind, and ushered me down the hall, into a large room. It was painfully sterile, with white brick walls, black and white checkered floor tiles, two fluorescent pendant light fixtures, and it reeked of disinfectant.

The orderly left, and I remained strapped to the gurney, half conscious, as my eyes rolled into a cloudy mist. Surreal Dali-like visions began to materialize, as haunting images of Charlie, Freddy, and the boys came screaming out of the darkness like an Edgar Allan Poe horror tale. Flames erupted all around me, as sweat oozed out of my body, only to be vaporized by the mounting inferno. The intense immolation was now burning *me,* along with my dead crew. *Had Judgment Day arrived!?* my mind screamed.

Suddenly, the apocalyptic hell storm ceased, as the horrifying image of the brain-eating monkeys returned! Strapped once again in vines, and helpless, I yelled, only to see a hazy figure rush through the throng of apes toward me. *Dear God!* I thought, *is this the alpha ape for real?* As the shadowy figure approached, with its blank face and a round shiny medallion on its forehead, it was apparent the apparition was humanoid. *Thank God,* I thought. *I couldn't endure another skull-slicing event like that again!*

The figure then spoke. "Relax, Tito. I'm Dr. Birnbaum. You're in good hands. I assure you, I *will* eradicate these traumatic hallucinations of yours."

As the vision before me fluctuated in and out of drifting veils of illusion, he continued, "We here at Allan VA Hospital are among the premiere scientists and surgeons in the country. We perform the most advanced procedures to address battle fatigue, and I am confident that this lobotomy *will* eliminate your pain."

My eyes widened, straining to focus on the doctor's face, when suddenly I noticed a deep scar running across his left cheek. As the man's deformed face came into focus, our eyes connected. "You're n-not Dr. Birnbaum, y-you're Metzger. Werner Metzger!"

"*Ja. Sehr gut!* Your vision and memory seem to be returning, Colonel Romano, but I will make sure they both recede into a world of utter darkness. So sit tight."

As I struggled to free my hands and legs, Metzger adjusted the reflector on his headband. He then turned to pick up a large hand auger, but opted for the electric surgical saw instead. Switching it on, Werner revved the motor, as the blade spun with an unnerving shriek. Metzger gazed at the blade and smiled. "This time you *will* pay for interrupting my critical biological research and for the scar on my face. It has been a constant reminder of the *dog* that clawed me, a dog that will now have its skull cut open so I can manipulate its intricate network of neurons and dendrites."

Turning toward me, Metzger gazed deep into my eyes. "I love my profession, Tito. What I had learned at Auschwitz has proven to be most useful here."

My eyes rolled, as I said with a slur, "You're n-no s-scientist, Metzger. You're a b-butcher!"

Werner laughed. "*Sehr gut,* once again, Tito, because Metzger actually means *butcher* in English." He paused and placed the saw down on the table as he pensively scratched his chin. "Interesting. I never gave that much thought." He chuckled.

"Apparently y-you don't g-give anything much thought," I retorted, "except barbarism! How the h-hell did they ever allow a m-mongrel like y-you to work here?"

Werner smiled as he sat on the stool next to me and drew his rolling equipment cart closer. With a firm kick, he locked the wheels in place, then clutched a razor and shaved all the hair off my head. With a blue marker, he drew his incision guidelines on my scalp, and finally replied, "*Ja,* it actually *is* rather bizarre, Colonel. Your country fought so valiantly to annihilate the Third Reich, claiming it to be a barbaric regime, yet here it is your haughty *civilized* nation leads the way in performing lobotomies, my specialty."

My lips twisted. "How can an ape like y-you know anything about t-the human mind? You Neanderthals even m-murdered your own people, deemed h-handicapped or u-useless."

Metzger chuckled. "That is quite humorous, Tito. But do you realize that it was an American, Samuel Williams, who first proposed the idea of euthanasia back in 1870? And Margaret Sanger also injected that concept into your society long before we Germans made good use of it."

I rolled my eyes. "If *you* w-were exterminated it would have been p-put to g-good use. But, *no*, you Nazi pigs had to m-murder millions of healthy p-prisoners out of p-pure ignorance and h-hatred."

Metzger shook his head, irritated. "Sentimental fools like you will simply never understand the plague to humanity that the Jews, gypsies, Slavs and other subhumans present, Tito. Nor will you ever comprehend the notions of survival of the fittest and the pursuit of knowledge. Hence, my critical work *must* continue, just like Wernher von Braun's, who I hear will soon be heading your new space administration. Wise Americans *have* embraced us superior Aryans, Tito, and Wernher's unrivalled knowledge of designing V1 and V2 rockets will also be put to good use. Of course, that's *if* he's wise enough to hold your nation hostage once he develops enough missiles to obliterate Washington, DC and Manhattan." Metzger grasped a syringe. "But first, here's a little more morphine to ease your pain before I begin sawing a nice little hole in your skull. After all, I'm not really a butcher, Tito. I take my scientific research very seriously."

"You're s-seriously deranged!" I managed to utter, as I felt the morphine surge through my veins and numb my senses.

Werner smiled, his creepy crooked teeth and wrinkled scar emanating a macabre specter of the hell soon to commence.

"Don't worry, Tito, I only gave you enough morphine to prohibit you from screaming in agony once I begin sawing into your skull. And believe me, it *is* pure agony. I know very well how patients scream when there isn't enough anesthesia." Werner snickered. "It's quite comical, actually, to see their eyes bulge out of their sockets as their bodies twist feverishly to break free from their shackles and the excruciating pain."

"You're s-sick!" I squeaked out. "You're j-just a s-soulless animal."

Werner smiled. "No, no, Tito. Animals never seek to torment or torture their prey. They are far more civil than humans. But you must view this procedure as expanding mankind's knowledge of the human brain. Although I will purposely tamper with your cerebellum to disconnect your ability to speak and then meddle with your memory—for security reasons, of course, and to satiate my thirst for revenge—the remainder of my experiments will be for the good of science. So, pat yourself on the back, Tito, you have donated your body to science."

"Unshackle m-my hands," I growled, "and I'll gladly p-pat my back…after I s-strangle *you!*"

Werner laughed. "I must say, in an odd way, I do actually like you, Tito. I admire your courage and resolve. It's quite German-like. But face it, *you lost!*" Werner's face contorted with vengeance as his voice reeked with animus. "So, shut the hell up and just lie still! I'm in control now. So, prepare to become a vegetable, Tito."

Werner turned on the surgical saw as the motor whirred, its piercing shrill echoing off the sterile chamber's walls. Adjusting the reflector on his headband, Metzger then steadied the saw with both hands and moved it toward the blue-marker lines on my bald scalp.

My eyes bulged and teeth clenched tight as I feverishly tried to break free of the leather straps. As I saw the spinning blade move out of sight, towards my scalp, I spit in Werner's face! Metzger flinched and the blade missed the mark, cutting a shallow gash just above my ear. Before Werner could blink away the spit, his head eerily snapped sideways. Metzger squealed in sheer agony as he dropped the saw and fell to the floor. Frantically, he reached for his head, only to feel a large familiar object embedded in his skull. He struggled to sit upright, then gazed up at his attacker. There, before his eyes, was Emily, standing above him with her eyes ablaze.

Werner labored to speak as blood gushed from his head and down his face, the large auger bit protruding out of his skull. "You! You f-filthy Jew b-bastard!"

Emily placed the pointy heel of her shiny red-leather pump on his chest, and spat, "*You*, you demented Nazi! What do *you* think about *my* experiment?"

With a hard thrust from her foot, Werner fell backward, his head hitting the floor as his eyes rolled. A puddle of blood pooled into an abstract shape of crimson goo, clashing with the geometric black-and-white floor tiles. With his last breath, Werner released a harrowing shriek of utter pain as his body violently convulsed, then went limp.

Emily rushed to my side and hurriedly unbuckled my restraints.

I gazed up at her through misty eyes, and murmured, "G-good God, Emmy. I c-can't believe w-what you did."

She swallowed hard as she placed a gauze pad on my oozing cut, then hugged me tight. "Well, you saved me from this menace at Auschwitz, so I guess I owed you."

Lovingly, I kissed her, then edged her away, gazing into her steadfast eyes. "But h-how did you know to c-come back?"

As she applied Iodine to the wound, she said, "As I was leaving, I overheard them say you were being prepped for a lobotomy." Emily's face twisted. "Can you believe that?

A lobotomy! What has become of this country?" she scoffed as she continued caring to my wound. "Naturally, I adamantly objected, yet the receptionist told me not to worry, that you had the most qualified doctor at the facility. She then showed me an article about Dr. Birnbaum in a recent medical journal. That's when my eyes caught a glimpse of Metzger's photograph. I could never forget the face of the Butcher of Birkenau."

I rubbed my baldhead. "Did you know metzger means *butcher* in English?"

"Yes," she said, as she gazed down at his dead body. "But it looks like Werner won't be butchering anyone else anymore."

I nodded with relief. "That's for s-sure."

With a sigh, I pulled Emily into my arms. "Well, so much for c-curing my head wound. I'm afraid *this* nightmare will just be added t-to all my others, haunting me f-for a lifetime."

Emily grasped the surgical saw. "Well, I *could* try cutting into that thick skull of yours to release the demons."

I smiled as I gazed down at Metzger's mutilated head. "Well, judging by your past efforts, I think you need a bit more practice, honey."

Emily dropped the saw and leaned in for a kiss. Then tenderly she rubbed my baldhead, and said, "How odd; now *I* have hair and *you're* bald."

"Well, I'd rather be bald than have Metzger or Chinese monkeys messing with my brain."

Emily squinted, confused, as a nurse entered the room, her eyes wide with shock. "What in God's name happened!?"

Emily and I turned toward her, as Emily said, "Please, call the police. It's a long story."

I rubbed my bruised head, and added, "Yes, and if you do care to listen, you'll need a chair and a stiff drink, because this chilling tale is one helluva mind bender."

KENNEDY: *Charismatic yet Reckless Leader*

A cold breeze tenderly massaged the unripe cherry buds along Pennsylvania Avenue. Sitting apprehensively in the Oval Office was John F. Kennedy. He had just received another injection in his lower back, containing amphetamines, to ease his perpetual infliction from both Addison's and venereal disease. Sitting with his eyes closed, he felt the potent drug surge through his veins, numbing his pain.

Moments earlier, a Secret Service agent had discreetly escorted one of his countless call girls out of his office. Thriving on the rush from the escapade and the drug, the president gravely contemplated his next encounter. It was March 22, 1962.

Walking purposefully down the corridor toward the president's office was FBI Director J. Edgar Hoover. Hoover was a meticulous and devoted officer who, during his total tenure, served under eight presidents, amounting to more than fifty years. After Charles Bonaparte (the Italian-American relative to Napoleon Bonaparte) founded the FBI, Edgar was immensely influential in the structuring and effectiveness of the bureau, yet Hoover had his own baggage as well. He harbored racial prejudices, engaged in various forms of corruption, and he had to keep his intimate relationship with his associate, Clyde Tolson, a secret.

Passing Hoover on his way out was Dr. Max Jacobson. Kicking back the pace of his terse gait, Hoover peered at the doctor, and barked sarcastically, "Ah, making another routine visit, Dr. Feelgood?"

The doctor mordantly smirked. "Stick it, Edgar!"

"Ah, yes. *Stick it,* like your poisonous syringe? No, not I, you druggie bastard!"

The doctor walked coldly past the director and quietly exited the building.

Hoover turned in disgust and grumbled, "I'll nail that beatnik's ass one day."

Doctor Feelgood's injections were even highly suspicious to Bobby Kennedy, who had the drugs tested by the FDA. When Bobby confronted his brother about the possible dangers, John remarked, "I don't care if it's horse piss, it works!" So the treatments continued.

Arriving precisely on time, Hoover rapped on the president's door.

"Enter," the president commanded.

Looking like a smashed-faced pug denied a meal, J. Edgar stormed through the door and entered the Oval Office.

Taken aback, the president responded tactfully, "Please, have a seat, Director. Relax."

Abruptly taking a seat, Hoover's agitated feet began tapping, as did his short stubby fingers on his knees. Hoover had always been clever and reserved, but this day his fuse seemed exceptionally short.

The president looked at him straight-faced, yet with an internal grin, gaining some pleasure from the director's agitation, as he inquired, "So, what's up? Is this some more commi nonsense about Martin Luther King?"

Hoover looked up and barked, "No! That damn pinko is another story. But since you asked, our wiretaps *did* record your friend's sinful, adulterous voice. The Reverend said, and I quote, 'Fucking is a form of anxiety reduction.'"

The president smiled, then nonchalantly leaned back—resting his chin on the palm of his hand.

Unhappy with the response, Hoover became even more volatile. "This is exactly what I mean! King is a tomcat with obsessive, degenerate sexual urges. He bangs women like a machinegun. And on that note, Mr. President, I must say that *you* and your brother make my job equally demanding. My patience and silence is nearing an end, so I'll be blunt. It was solely due to your father that I maintain any sense of restraint, and — "

"Director," the president interjected, as he leaned tersely forward. "Feel free to choose any path you damn well please. Your patience or allegiance to my father is of little concern to Bobby or me. We both love and respect our father more than words can say, and fully appreciate all that his efforts and connections have done for us. But make no mistake, Bobby and I are new blood. So my advice to you is...choose your words and position very carefully."

Hoover sprung to his feet, and planted both of his thick paws firmly on the president's desk. "Listen, Johnny, your father and I go way back, old school. And even though I detest many things he did, we still managed to see it clear to pull together in some fashion. I'm fully aware that it was upon your father's advice that you retained me in this position, but now it's *my* turn to give *you* some advice. You, and your little brother, are playing with fire. You should know that my loyalty is matched only by my diligence and moral code. I have reliable information that can easily strip the mangy fur right off your bony backs! I could have a field day plastering your salacious Kennedy-pelts in every tabloid across the nation."

Kennedy leaned back with a cocky grin, and retorted, "What in God's name are you talking about?"

"Do I look green, like you two shady shamrocks? I know about your countless liaisons with numerous party girls and celebrities, like Angie Dickinson and Lee Remick, not to mention your obscured marriage to Durie Malcolm. I have a file on you dating back to the forties. But, most important, is your suicidal affiliation with Sammy Giancana. We know that Judy Campbell Exner is more than just another pretty face. She's a conduit between you two, delivering dirty money, and then gratifying you both with dirty deeds. She's just a double-dealing tramp, and I'm sure she transported your father's payoffs that got you elected. So, if you're foolish enough to mess with hoods like Giancana and Johnny Rosselli, you'll see what will happen if you cut me and my department out."

"Director, I appreciate your concern, but I'm a big boy and can handle myself. Besides—"

"Big boy, my ass!" Hoover intrepidly interjected. "You don't have a damn clue as to what or whom big boys really are. Do you?"

Kennedy folded his arms firmly. "Edgar, I was raised by a titan that parlayed one success into another, and all the while dealing with the most affluent, intelligent, and even barbaric of men. If you think Bobby or I are afraid of the mob, you're sadly mistaken. Besides, we have no dealings with them. Yes, the CIA at one time did under Eisenhower, but we are not that sort of administration."

Hoover looked at the president with his cold and distrusting pug eyes. "Mr. President, you know I'm loyal, but I will not sit idly by if I catch wind of any actions or behaviors that will soil the name of this great office. The entire country's reputation rides upon your every action, so proceed with care, and try to show some restraint."

"Once again, Director, I appreciate your concern. But I assure you everything is under control. The Kennedy family is very resilient."

Hoover stood erect, and retorted wryly, "Well, you may have been able to buy your way into office, but be careful! You just might buy a bullet that will put you permanently out of office."

Hoover turned, and began to exit the Oval Office, as the president replied calmly, "Thanks for the advice. Have a good day, Director, and just make sure to keep your superior, the Attorney General, informed of anything new."

With a grimace, Hoover turned toward the president, paused, and then groaned. "Like I said, your baby brother better watch his ass, too! You Kennedy boys are like horny little rabbits frolicking atop Mt. Vesuvius. I'm telling you, don't get the Mafia pissed off. Or they'll erupt and roast both of your cotton-tailed asses!"

Swiveling about, Hoover stormed out the door and slammed it shut.

The president then leaned over and pressed his intercom to summon his secretary, Evelyn Lincoln. "Evelyn, please hold all my calls, I'm going down to the pool. My brothers are stopping by for a dip."

"Yes, sir. Is there anything special you or your brothers need?"

"No, just the usual."

The president hastily exited his office and scurried down the hall toward the pool. En route, he ran into Kenny O'Donnell.

O'Donnell stopped in his tracks. "How did your meeting go, Mr. President? I just saw J. Edgar storm into the restroom, and he didn't look too happy."

The president slowed down. "Oh, the old wind bag blew his stack, just like a whiny little wench. But I guess I scared the piss out of him!" As O'Donnell grinned, the president added, "I bet he needs to squat to pee!"

O'Donnell burst out laughing. "But seriously, do we need to be worried?"

The president smiled. "Hell, no! *J. Edna* is no problem."

O'Donnell shook his head laughing, as they parted ways.

The president eventually made his way to the pool's private locker room. Hastily stripping down to his bare bones, he tossed his suit on a hook and grabbed a towel.

Whipping the towel around his neck, the president then strut into the pool area. Ted and Bobby were already skinny-dipping with four attractive young women. Laughing and splashing about, their Bostonian accents reverberated off the tile walls and floor, giving the president a sense of home. "Hey, Teddy boy," John said, "so you're aiming for my Senate seat, huh. Would you jump in my grave that fast?"

Teddy smiled as he whipped his head back to shake the water out of his hair. "Jump into your grave, no! But in *this* pool, hell yeah!" he said, as he pinched the naked girl's buttocks beside him.

John tossed his towel on a chair and walked to the pool's edge, his toes gripping the coping. "Well, be careful, because they'll be looking up your ass with a microscope when you start running for office. And they'll also probably want to know why you dropped out of Harvard."

Bobby laughed as he looked at his younger brother. "Yeah, so will you tell the press it was because you cheated on an exam, you damn knucklehead?"

Ted frowned as he cupped his hand and whipped his arm across the water, splashing his brother in the face. Bobby chuckled and dove under, while John glanced poolside.

Sitting butt-naked on a lounge chair was Dave Powers, the president's trusted aide who arranged these frequent sessions. With a smile, the much older Powers waved to the young chief, as a wet young blonde sat on his lap.

Outside, Secret Service agents Don Puglisi and Harry Newman nervously paced the perimeter. As the young agents had dreaded, a feisty old cabinet member was hurriedly approaching the locked doors. Brimming with urgency, he cried, "I need to speak with the president at once! Is he here?"

Puglisi stepped forward. "Yes, but you know the drill, he can't be disturbed."

"Jesus Christ! That's just great. So, you're telling me that important matters of state have to wait, while he frolics in the pool?"

"I guess so," Puglisi replied.

The crafty old official anxiously pulled out a pack of Lucky Strikes, peeled open the corner and shook three cigarettes halfway out. He offered them to Puglisi, but the savvy agent refused.

"Come on, son! There's no way you can get me in there?"

Puglisi stood firm and crossed his arms. The official looked at the floor, and shook his head in disbelief. Then sticking the cigarette between his lips, he snapped it lit with his Zippo, and turned about. As he chugged away, mumbling curses under his heated breath, he emitted a long trail of smoke, like a fiery steam engine.

Puglisi feverishly pivoted toward Newman. "This is bullshit! Here we are, sworn to protect the most powerful leader in the world, while he padiddles with a couple of bimbos."

Newman frowned. "Hell yeah, and I can't even keep track of how many gals he's hopped into bed with. The guy's an animal."

Puglisi smirked. "Yeah, a horny marsupial! Who knows how many pouches he filled with his offspring?"

Newman laughed. "Don't even talk like that. Imagine a whole mob of illegitimate Kennedys hopping around? No thanks!"

Puglisi shook his head. "Yeah, that would be enough to make even Captain Kangaroo cry!"

Newman cracked up as he scratched his peach-fuzz crew cut. "You're a pisser, Puglisi!" Yet as he rubbed his chin, a disturbed frown etched his face. "But what really ticks me off is that we don't even know who these broads are. That dirt bag, Powers, just struts right by us with these babes, from God knows where, and all without clearance of any kind."

"Yeah, let's just hope these dames know how to keep quiet or never get pregnant. Or even worse, never lure the president into an ambush."

Newman sighed. "Jesus, you're right; this could get ugly or even deadly."

"No shit! We have no clue as to who these dames are. They could be communist spies, or God knows what? Christ, half of them speak with an accent, and the Cold War is escalating on every front. Berlin, Korea, Cuba, Vietnam, this is crazy. I feel like a praetorian guard for Caligula."

Newman pulled out a crumbled pack of Old Golds and popped a white cylinder into his mouth. As he lit up, he mumbled, "Well, let's just hope this Dave Powers guy can be trusted."

Puglisi shook his head. "I doubt it; he's just a glorified pimp. And this president needs to get on the ball, not constantly have one. I can just see it now; as one broad drinks a Harvey Wallbanger, another has a session with Johnny Whorebanger."

Newman laughed. "Yeah, well, at least now I know what the 'F' in the middle of Kennedy's name stands for!"

❄ ❄ ❄

Despite this scene being fictional it was based upon many facts, such as President Kennedy's afflictions, Dr. Feelgood's drug injections, Kennedy's connection with the Mafia, his liaisons with over a hundred women—many of whom were complete strangers—and his skinny-dipping sexcapades.

Moreover, Kennedy's dialogue was fitted with direct quotes, such as the "horse piss" line and the sarcastic remarks about J. Edgar Hoover, such as calling him "J. Edna," and "I bet he needs to squat to pee."

Hoover's outrage and his verbal slurs to Kennedy were created, yet the intel he conveyed was factual and known to him and the FBI. Hoover's "tomcat" remark about Martin Luther King was a direct quote, as was Martin Luther King's vulgar, sexual F-bomb comment, which *was* recorded by the FBI. (Note: The photo above was Photoshoped. Edgar's head was placed on Nikita Khrushchev's body, which had a similar hefty frame.)

Additionally, although Secret Service agent Don Puglisi was fictional, real-life agent Joseph Paolella faced similar situations. Agent Paolella was torn; he was proud to be the first Italian-American to become a Secret Service agent, but was humiliated by his first presidential assignment. Sworn to protect the president from danger with his own life, he was soon left guarding the privacy of a reckless, party animal with an unquenchable libido.

Years later, doctors realized that some of the pain-killing drugs that Kennedy had been taking further enhanced his already over-active sex drive. However, the president had a stronger sex-drug running through his veins, and that was the blood of a true Kennedy, inherited from his father, Joe.

However, despite President Kennedy's negative traits, he was very successful in his showdown with the USSR during the Cuban Missile Crisis, and his charisma and uplifting speeches, particularly his call for America to put a man on the moon before the decade was out, did have a profound and positive effect on the nation. Many Americans from both parties regard Kennedy as having been an effective president despite his personal flaws. His tragic death was a shock to all and remains enshrouded in mystery.

BORGIAS: *The Pernicious Pope and Devious Duke*

A swirling wind blew across the Tuscan hills, twisting the towering cypress trees like a manic Van Gogh painting. In the midst of this gale stood Duke Cesare Borgia and his newly appointed military engineer, Leonardo da Vinci.

Leonardo was highly recommended to Cesare by many who had witnessed his magnificent works of art, mastery of mathematical perspective, and seemingly infinite array of interests. They had also informed Cesare of da Vinci's secret obsession with engineering and science, coupled with an impressive gift for invention.

Cesare's military successes were like a magnet that drew talent, and money was no object. Being the illegitimate son of the immensely powerful Pope Alexander VI, Cesare had few financial worries and could easily compensate his personnel.

Wearing his flamboyant black beret with a white plume, the Duke haughtily approached Leonardo, as his military entourage marched close behind.

"So, Leonardo, I am told you can perform miracles, not only with oils, but with engineering and math, as well."

"Duca, everything in nature is composed of mathematical elements."

Cesare smiled. "Yes, like the number of cities I conquer, the rivals I kill, or the amount of taxes I collect!"

Cesare's soldiers looked at their leader with pride as they released a hearty barrage of sinister cackles.

"No! Not human nature," Leonardo replied. "Nature itself."

A silence quickly befell Cesare and his men as they all simultaneously turned toward Leonardo.

"Go on, *continui,*" Cesare commanded.

"Duca, I have studied Aristotle, and conversed with many of our greatest mathematical minds at the University of Padua. However, most important, are my own studies that have revealed many truths about nature. Its immense and complex construction, at its most minuscule level, is actually built upon elements of mathematical proportions. I have yet to figure out those equations, but they all fit together in various combinations forming an infinite variety of wondrous matter, which our eyes perceive daily. Yet, most are blind to these glorious doorways to knowledge. Instead, they rely upon the speculation, and oft-repeated verbiage of others, without looking or experimenting for themselves. *Ignoranza,* I tell you, the world is plagued with ignorance!"

Cesare's men looked at one another, unsure of how to react, until one bellowed, "What the hell did he just say?"

Igniting a guffaw, the garrison sounded like a wild bunch of donkeys, until Cesare blasted, "You damn idiots, *silenzio*! He obviously speaks of you!"

Lowering their heads, like scolded dogs, the soldiers stood, uneasy and even more baffled. As Cesare turned to address Leonardo, one of the soldiers spotted a man on horseback in the distance. The unmarked rider was heading their way and now began charging up the hill.

"Cesare, someone approaches!" the soldier exclaimed.

Instinctively, the armored watchdogs all wielded their swords as all heads turned toward the intruder.

Cesare turned, and barked, "He rides alone, stand down!"

Breaking into a leaping stride, the horse chewed up grass and gravel with his hooves as he made his way up the steep hillside. The muscular Spanish mustang feverishly approached, then stopped tersely as his rider urgently tugged back on the reins.

Trying to steady his horse, the rider announced, "Pope Alexander VI has summoned the immediate presence of Duca Cesare Borgia."

One of the soldiers boldly approached the rider and growled, "This better be an official summons."

"It is, sir, it is!"

Upon receiving the document the soldier carefully inspected the scroll's wax papal seal. He knew that the pope's *pescatorio,* or Fisherman's Ring, doubled as a signet ring that left a unique impression in the sealing wax. Looking back at Cesare, the soldier nodded, confirming its authenticity.

Cesare smiled. "Yes, I know he's official."

The soldier squinted. "But how? He wears no official colors. Do you know him, my Lord?"

Cesare grinned and shook his head. "No, no, I could tell by the horse he's riding. The mustang is my father's favorite from the old country; España."

Cesare then cocked his head, gazing over at da Vinci. "My father beckons me, Leonardo, so I must depart. But as I had previously informed you, it is imperative that you survey this entire region and render precise maps. They are crucial to our plotting future campaigns. Terrain plays an important role in military strategy. Something many fools ignore. So precision, Leonardo, is paramount."

"You need not worry, *il mio* Duca. In addition to supplying you with the best maps your eyes shall ever see I shall also show you designs for military weapons and fortifications no mind has ever envisioned or thought imaginable."

Cesare smiled. "From the impressive recommendations by my compatriots I trust you will indeed surprise and please me, Leonardo. Be well, and don't hesitate to ask for anything you may need in fulfilling your task." Cesare then leaned over and whispered, "Even if it means muzzles for these buffoons!"

Leonardo laughed, and then thanked his new patron. The headstrong leader swiftly mounted his horse, and with a terse tug, quickly swiveled about. Designating two of his men as escorts, Cesare then motioned to the messenger to take the lead. With their spurs pricking their horses' loins, the quartet briskly departed for Rome.

The restless evening sky grew even darker as gloomy purple clouds choked the last remnants of cobalt out of the atmosphere. Thunder rumbled in the distance as veins of lightning ripped through the heavens. Riding up toward the recently built Sistine Chapel, erected previously by Pope Sixtus IV, the messenger pointed to the chapel's door. "That is where the pope wishes to meet you. He commanded that you go alone."

Cesare motioned for his men to stay put as his eyes surveyed the area. Slowly, he dismounted his horse and tethered it to a post. As Cesare cautiously advanced, a bolt of lightning suddenly illuminated the structure. Cesare looked up, his upper lip twisting as he released a subtle grunt. The chapel's mundane façade did not impress. Continuing forward, Cesare finally reached the arched doorway.

As the howling winds ravaged the trees, Cesare pushed open the door and entered the dark chapel. Taking only two steps, he then used his back to close the wind-blown door, keeping his eyes glued to the dark and silent interior before him. He was soon struck by the pungent scent of the two fragrant candles some twenty feet away—their tiny flickering flames struggling to illuminate even the smallest sections of the vast chamber. Gazing up at the unadorned plaster walls and high vaulted ceiling, Cesare was overwhelmed by a macabre sense of being ensnared in a vacant tomb. Cautiously, Cesare took small halfhearted steps when suddenly a faint metallic sound irritated his eardrum.

Cesare soon realized that the culprit was a squeaky set of door hinges, emanating from the far side of the chamber. As his eyes squinted to focus, a dark rotund figure appeared in the doorway. Flanking the huge silhouette were two slim figures, each bearing an oil lamp.

Astutely aware of deadly coups, Cesare slowly placed his right hand over his sword's pearl-inlaid handle. As the three figures approached, their footsteps icily reverberated throughout the empty chamber. Cesare vigilantly glanced to the left, then right, his keen peripheral vision even managing to scan his back. Slowly, the obscure silhouettes began to emerge from the darkness.

Then the familiar voice of his father finally signaled, "Is that you, my son?"

With a sigh of relief, Cesare replied, "Yes, father, it is I…Cesare." With a smile, he calmly lowered his sweaty hand and wiped it on his trousers.

The pope, majestically adorned in a bejeweled vestment, at last appeared. His broad face, lit by the flickering lamps below, produced a sinister effect that at first startled Cesare.

Then the pope smiled and extended his hand, revealing the golden *pescatorio*. Cesare respectfully lowered his head and kissed his father's ring.

"It has been far too long, Cesare."

"Yes, father, it has, but indeed we're both busy men, and share the same responsibilities."

The pope's two clergymen recoiled with offense as one intrusively lifted his lamp to illuminate Cesare's face. In a voice reeking with consternation, he declared, "Young man, you are addressing the pope! How dare you compare your actions to his Eminence? Show some respect!"

Sensing Cesare's blood about to boil, Alexander quickly interjected, "Please, my son is a very spirited stallion. We are in private quarters and his words here are spoken not to a pope, but to his father."

"Your Eminence, with all due respect, we are fully aware of Cesare's lineage, but we must also advise you, as is our duty, that such practices spawn repetition and, as such, will repeat themselves in public. It is blasphemous for Cesare to think his station equals yours. He must learn obedience. After all, Your Holiness, you are our Lord's most exalted here on earth, you are the vicar and overseer of the Holy See."

Before Alexander could reply, Cesare exploded, "You mangy little flea! You best *wholly see* this!" Cesare unexpectedly snuffed the clergyman's candle out with his two bare fingers, and continued, "Beware of my powers, priest. Your pious words may control the delusional masses, but certainly not me. For I know very well the truth of our existence, and you're both just charlatans! Remember this, we are all made of flesh and blood…for if I were to slit your throats, blood would surely flow, not the symbolic wine or wrath of your ancient God. You see, my little vermin, it's just that I, like my father, have the balls to seize opportunity in this earthly domain. That his rule falls under the banner of

God, and mine under a coat of arms, makes absolutely no difference, no difference at all! *Capisca?!"*

As the other clergyman attempted to squeak out a reply, Cesare quickly plunged his deadly index finger into his chest. "And the ones who should learn obedience are the insignificant fleas like you! Who at their best can only survive by clinging onto their all-powerful host. So, let me shatter your fragile delusions, both of you. It is leaders like *us* who rule this domain. So, shut up and enjoy the ride!"

Alexander finally took action. "Cesare, *basta!* Your temper has always been like Vesuvius. It will reap the same deadly results one day if you don't learn to harness it. And, my son, despite the madness that reigns here on earth, I firmly believe in our Lord Jesus Christ. So, for the sake of our heavenly Father and your earthly father, please, show some respect."

"Father, you know I will not tolerate being reprimanded by feeble little insects. If I offended you, father, forgive me. But as for them…to hell with them! I have killed real men for less, men sheathed in rigid bronze armor and wielding razor-sharp daggers, not feeble little fairies like this, who flutter about in flimsy cassocks. Perhaps we should speak alone, man-to-man, without these damn pesky fleas hovering about and whining in my ear."

Alexander's face turned red. "Cesare, I now command you…*basta!* (Enough!) And that, my son, comes from no feeble little flea! For your life's blood, in body and estate, is very much under my influence." Glancing at his two escorts, he added, "And as for you two, perhaps it is best you leave us. I have many important things to discuss with Cesare, and we have all wasted precious time."

Seething in silence, the two clergymen made an about-face and proceeded toward the exit. Disgusted by Cesare's lack of respect and the pope's tainted lifestyle, their minds began reeling in humiliation.

They each saw this whole debacle as the fruition of Alexander's many transgressions, which they were forced to bear in silence. Sure they enjoyed the power and prestige of being the pope's aides, but they couldn't stomach the entourage, which in private they chided as the Barbaric Borgia Brigade. They loathed being constantly reminded and incensed by Alexander's power politics and shameful indiscretions. The pope made no attempt to conceal his many children, and he flagrantly flaunted his many love affairs. Such as his latest scandal, where he had the portrait of his mistress made to look like the Virgin Mary, then mounted it over his bedchamber's door.

In desperation, one of the clergymen's eyes rolled upward as he silently prayed, *Dear Lord, please end this sacrilegious nightmare!*

As they passed through the chapel's exit, they eagerly slammed the door behind them without even turning their heads. Continuing their forward trajectory, they tenaciously kept their backs to what they knew was a repugnant mess.

Secluded in the dark chapel, Alexander lit a wall-mounted candle and slowly turned back toward his son. "Cesare, you know I have always done my best to make up for the lost time I could never spend with you as a boy."

Cesare nodded as his father continued, "I have consistently supported your efforts, and I do so because I have full faith in your abilities. Likewise, you have repeatedly shown that my investment, financially and affectionately, was sound. So I never wish to see outbursts like that again when you're on papal grounds."

"Very well, father, but then don't summon me here anymore. Let's meet on neutral ground from here forward."

"Cesare, you really are a stubborn bastard!"

"Indeed I am, Papa, on both accounts!"

Father and son burst out laughing and warmly embraced. Their acknowledging smiles confirmed that the spoiled apple indeed doesn't fall far from the rotten tree.

Alexander then stepped back as his paternal smile vanished. "My son, I have some very critical tasks that I can only entrust to you. Two of my bishops have conveniently passed away. Long story short, they were nosey pains in the ass, but I need you to secure all their possessions and properties."

Cesare looked at his father with a sinister smile. "Has father done something naughty?"

Alexander rolled his eyes. "No, no, the old farts died naturally. Listen! Obviously, this must be executed in a most discreet fashion. I need you to sell off their estates to friends or close associates of ours so as not to arouse the clergy or congregation's suspicions. Try to secure a maximum price, as those proceeds, my son, will help fund your campaigns in the Romagna."

A devious grin etched Cesare's face. "Consider it done."

"But Cesare, please understand the broader picture here. Almost two hundred years ago, Pope Clement V moved the papacy to France, where it lasted for a hundred years. Over that time Rome lost control over much of its people and territory," as Alexander continued, his face reddened with rage, "that is intolerable and will not stand! Moreover, let us not forget how King Charles of France made his advances to remove me, or should I say *us* Borgias, just a few years ago. Fortunately, his concern over the reaction of the people thwarted his efforts, for we were never so close to losing our heads. So, we must take this very seriously."

As dutiful son nodded, doting father continued, "However, I have been making some headway with King Ferdinand of Spain, and we might be able to gain a sizeable foothold on some new and possibly fertile territories across the Atlantic Ocean, as well."

Cesare's covetous eyes widened. "Holy shit! That's fantastic!"

Alexander shook his head. "Must you continue to act like a horse's ass in God's house?"

Cesare shrugged his shoulders, but then his eyebrows suddenly lifted. "Speaking of horses and Ferdinand, I hear the king has that Columbus fellow shipping your favorite Spanish mustangs over to the new world."

Alexander nodded. "Yes, it's a great animal. I'm sure it will come in handy over there, as no horses exist there."

"Indeed. And I absolutely love Mustangs. They outrun the best of the rest and have great stamina. I see you outfitted your messenger with one."

Alexander nodded. "Yes, and I can also see why you like them, because they're a bit like you—wild!"

Father and son grinned, yet Alexander's face quickly regained gravity. "Never mind the mustangs, Cesare, remember, we must regain control of these wayward city-states all around us. They have deplorably abandoned the one and true papacy here in Rome. You shall indeed govern over all these provinces, Cesare, but they must be reunited with their true nation state and religious obligations. Rome must not lose its iron grip. Rome's survival, and more importantly, our family's survival depend on it!"

The two tightly embraced, then started to walk toward the chapel's exit. As their footsteps echoed in the cavernous chamber, Cesare peered about. "You know, father, I hate to bring up horses again, but this chapel looks like a stable. Someday you should have it decorated, perhaps with a nice fresco. It's really rather cold and depressing in here."

The pope smiled. "Yes, perhaps you're right, my son." Alexander gazed up at the cracked and bumpy masonry as they approached the exit. "After all, an illusionary fresco would nicely conceal the ugly rock underneath."

❄ ❄ ❄

As time would tell, the avaricious Borgias did nothing to decorate the Sistine Chapel; that would occur under Pope Julius II when he commissioned Michelangelo to decorate the ceiling, thus turning a vacant, cold chamber into a glowing masterpiece. However, despite the magnificence of the illusionary fresco, it could never truly hide the ugly rock underneath—namely the reprehensible deeds of ignoble popes like Alexander and his Borgia brigade who brought shame upon sacred ground—for truth always bleeds through camouflage, eventually.

Despite this vignette being fictional, the events incorporated within it were mostly factual. Leonardo was indeed hired by Cesare Borgia as a military engineer and did create maps for the Duke, which were meticulously detailed aerial maps that exceeded most efforts of official mapmakers of the time. Likewise, the devious machinations discussed by the pernicious pope and his devious ducal son were factual, as the Borgia brigade had left an indelible stain on the Holy See, a dark and odious one that the entire world could wholly see.

EDISON & TESLA: *The Electro Age*

Relentless winds swept over the rolling seas of the North Atlantic, as its biting chill froze the decks of *L'Amérique*. En route to New York, the famous actress, Sarah Bernhardt, stepped out of the steamship's coal-heated cabin to encounter the raw elements. Being an adventurous soul, Sarah wanted to smell the salty air and admire the untamed seas. As gas lamps flickered inside the ship's hull, cylindrical beams of light radiated out through a series of portholes, each being eerily truncated by the darkness of night.

The sultry diva buttoned her topcoat and gazed back toward the ship's stern. Sarah was immediately awestruck at how the massive eastern-horizon vanished into a black void. It was as if the ship were sailing amid the abyss of deep space. Turning about, Sarah cemented her footing and wrapped her thick scarf around her neck. As the ship pitched and rolled, Sarah unsteadily began walking toward the bow. The cold, salty air chilled her warm lungs as she clutched the bow's frigid railing. With great anticipation, Sarah gazed upon the western horizon. The distant silhouette of the New World was backlit by a faint, yet warm and shimmering glow. With an inner calm, Sarah raised her leather-clad hands in front of her face, then exhaled, hoping to defrost her now frozen face. Yet the paltry warmth emanating from her tiny lungs was instantly consumed by the huge oceanic air mass. Her discomfort, however, was quickly abated when she saw the towering silhouettes of Manhattan's skyline. It was late November of 1880.

As the steamship *L'Amérique* entered New York's harbor, it quietly sailed past the vacant spot that in six years would host America's colossal icon, the Statue of Liberty. As the ocean liner reached port, Sarah grasped her bag and disembarked.

Not far from the cold harbor, on the Jersey mainland, was Menlo Park. It was the famed site of the inventive wizard Thomas Alva Edison. Sitting behind his oil-stained desk, the prematurely gray-haired alchemist scribbled diagrams with illegible notations, resembling a Da Vinci codex.

Stepping into his office to summon the mastermind was Robert Cutting, a company trustee, who took it upon himself to act as interpreter for their surprise guest. "Mr. Edison, I have a special visitor from Europe that I know you'll be delighted to meet."

"Well, show him in, Robert."

"Sir, it is not a man, but a woman, and a famous woman at that!"

"Okay then, very well. Show *her* in!"

With histrionic flare, Cutting announced, "Ladies and gentlemen, may I introduce the ultimate stage-sensation of our time…Sarah Bernhardt!"

Edison's head recoiled as he dropped the carbon element that was in his hand.

Strolling seductively through the factory's office door, the world-renowned diva graciously smiled at her astonished host. Edison leapt to his feet and coyly flipped back the wayward hairs that traversed his wide face. Instinctively, he wiped his filthy hands on his homemade lab smock and cracked a nervous smile. As Sarah approached, the perceptive inventor observed how her golden curls of hair bounced like illuminated coils of filament.

With a grin, he extended his dirty, carbon-stained hand, as the gracious diva clasped it with both of hers, tactfully concealing her relief that her hands remained sheltered under her black leather gloves.

As Sarah eloquently spoke in French, Robert Cutting dutifully translated the diva's words. "I have anticipated this moment for quite some time, Mr. Edison. I hold you in very high esteem, and I'm enchanted by your bold assertion. Namely, to illuminate New York City with your incandescent light bulbs."

"Bold assertion, indeed," Edison said. "I'm pleased that you said *assertion*, Mrs. Bernhardt, and not *fanciful claim*, or some other derogatory remark that I see printed in the papers these days. I've been working on perfecting this confounded invention for several years now, quite longer than anticipated. But it won't be long now."

Once again Cutting relayed Sarah's response. "I must say that I am impressed by your creativity, but I did hear that your incandescent bulb was actually invented a year earlier by British inventor Joseph Swan."

Edison's eyes rolled. "My dear woman, perhaps the papers have polluted your mind after all. One must remember that to invent something that is not implemented in society is of no value! Did you know that George Stephenson actually invented the locomotive ten years before the final model that now floods the market? Or that my perfection of Bell's telephone, by adding two carbon buttons fashioned out of lampblack, made it truly useable?"

Unnerved, Sarah stood glaring at Edison's vigorous reaction, while Cutting's tongue rattled to keep pace with the translation. After Edison's brief lecture, Sarah tactfully replied, "I apologize if I upset you, Mr. Edison, but it seems that pure invention is one thing, while improving ideas and bringing to market is quite another."

Edison's lips curled. "Well, invention is an enigma in itself. I have often said, 'Genius is one percent inspiration and ninety-nine percent perspiration.' Look at your prowess on the stage, Madame. You are adulated for the spectacular performances you create. Yet, did you not simply read the lines of a silent partner?" Sarah was taken aback, as Edison continued, "Yes, *the author*, who gets little or no credit at all and, most likely, fewer financial rewards as well. On the other hand, are not those lines but mute without *your* creative gifts to give them life? Where would you be without the author, or the author without you? So, did you not bring to market another's work? Therefore, in most instances, it is not just a singular action, but a progressive, or team, effort."

Sarah stood pensive as Cutting relayed the remaining translation. She then placed her black-leathered hands on her hips, and responded in her flamboyant French accent, as Cutting translated, "Yes, Mr. Edison, your clever analogy *is* quite interesting, not to mention cunning. Now I can see why you are so successful...you proficiently get right to the heart of the matter!"

Edison smiled. "Thank you, Mrs. Bernhardt. I'll take that as a compliment. You see, in the final analysis, bringing a product to market is the ultimate goal. Therefore, anything that won't sell, I don't want to invent. Its sale is proof of utility, and utility is success."

With a waving gesture, Edison thoughtlessly turned his back and began walking toward the factory's main laboratory. Sarah looked at Cutting, who then anxiously grasped her hand and quickly escorted the diva behind the eccentric wizard. Edison swung open the lab door and entered. But then he stopped suddenly and stepped back out. Realizing his lapse of etiquette, he turned and with an absentminded smile, waved for his guest to enter.

This elicited a smile from the diva, as she politely uncoupled her hand from Cutting's and proceeded forward. As she flowed past, in her lavish black gown, Edison glanced at Cutting and shrugged his shoulders, admitting his faux pas. Cutting winked, and the two men cordially followed.

Sarah looked around the huge laboratory, which was manned by six electrical engineers and twelve technicians. Generators, coils, armatures, and wires were haphazardly strewn all about. Two small gas lamps lit the rear, brick wall, while long tables lined with test bulbs proudly radiated their electrical discharge. Sarah was elated by the intense glow, and quickly turned with an equally radiant smile.

"Magnifique!" Sarah bellowed in her fanciful French tongue.

Yet as Edison grinned, several filaments snapped under heat distress. Instantly, the room dimmed. With a grimace, Edison retorted, "You see, one percent inspiration and ninety-nine percent perspiration!"

Sarah laughed, then perceptively conveyed her sentiments via Cutting, "Yes, I can now see. Inventing solutions to overcome repetitious failures must take the patience of a saint. Nay, in your case, this noble quest elevates you to an even higher station. For without doubt, you are like the mighty Prometheus. Against the will of the gods you have brought light to mankind!"

As two lab technicians dutifully attended the failed bulbs, Edison gazed at Sarah. "Well, Madame, your divine gifts for drama are duly noted. However, I must confess; I'm rather displeased with your mythological connotation. Prometheus *stole* fire from the heavens and gave it to mankind, whereas my countless hours and years of hard labor are in no way stealing, Madame."

Cutting glared at Edison, failing to translate his retort. He then whispered in English, "Thomas! Is it truly necessary to tell her *that*? She meant it as a lofty compliment."

Edison was briefly bewildered by Cutting's interjection, as his eyes darted from Sarah to his trusty translator. He paused, then waved his hand. "Ah, heck no, Robert! Just tell her I'm grateful. But, do tell her that I have something very special that she must see!"

Cutting cheerfully conveyed the revised message as Edison once again pressed on toward another room. Meanwhile, Sarah and Cutting followed, looking like two humble apprentices in a sorcerer's workshop. This time Edison remembered his manners, and courteously stood by the doorway, while Cutting escorted Sarah into the next lab room. There, on a table, stood an oddly shaped contraption with a huge funnel projecting curiously upward.

Sarah's smile swiftly transformed into a visual icon of bewilderment.

Getting a charge from Sarah's expression, Edison then positioned her near the strange device. Gazing deep into her eyes, he said, "This is an invention that will truly take your breath away. All you need to do is take a single strand of your hair and drop it into the magic funnel."

Upon hearing Cutting's translation, Sarah looked even more befuddled. "So, Mr. Rumpelstiltskin, does this machine spin hair into gold?"

Edison chuckled. "Very charming, Madame, but *no*. Please proceed."

Hesitantly, Sarah plucked a strand of her golden locks and looked at Edison. The wizard cracked a bizarre smile, then nodded that it was safe to proceed. Sarah turned, then skeptically dropped the hair into the funnel. Filled with anticipation, she watched it slide all the way down and disappear.

Edison then instructed, "Very well, Mrs. Bernhardt, now please make a wish. But speak *loudly*."

Sarah squinted, feeling as if she were in a tarot salon. Apprehensively, she incanted, *"Mai l'éclat léger!"*

While Sarah waited for a miraculous event to occur, she failed to notice Edison's mischievous hands behind his back, as he took a disc and placed it on the machine. While Sarah stared fixedly into the huge funnel—looking like a bewildered dog—a loud voice blared out of the funnel, intoning *"Mai l'éclat léger!"*

Sarah recoiled in amazement! She instantly recognized the voice; it was none other than her own! Dumbfounded, she cried, "What in blazes is this!? An echo machine?"

Edison and Cutting burst out laughing as Edison replied, "Sorry, Madame, but no. It is my pet invention, which I call a phonograph. You needn't use a strand of hair, for that was just a gag. However, this little gem records speech or any sound onto a foil plate, which can then be played back. I foresee many great uses for this device. Just think, we can now document the actual voices of great innovators, politicians, artists, singers and, naturally, many other great matters of historical importance."

Sarah listened carefully as Cutting decoded Edison's prophetic words. Her face suddenly beamed. "This is fantastic! Speaking of which, wouldn't it be grand to record Hector Berlioz's *Symphonie Fantastique*? Imagine; one can now listen to it without traveling to the Symphony Hall. Or one can collect all the great operas and plays, and replay them at their own convenience. May I try it again?"

"Be my guest. But this time would you honor me by reciting some lines from *Phèdre?"*

Sarah happily obliged, and once again the miraculous machine recorded and played back her dramatic voice. As a surprise, Sarah then recited a few lines from her upcoming play.

"Ah yes!" Edison exclaimed. "That's from *Hernani!* I'm a staunch admirer of Hugo's work, along with Verdi's scintillating operas, but alas, you knew that." As Sarah nodded, he added, "And your voice resonates quite well. Beautiful, Madame, simply beautiful!"

"Thank you," she replied. "As you know, that is from my role of Doña Sol. You are more than welcome to come as my guest to my next performance in Boston."

"Thank you, Mrs. Bernhardt, but as you can see, I am hopelessly married to my work. If, by chance, I get this darn light bulb to function properly, then perhaps."

Sarah demurely nodded, realizing the different worlds she and the scientist-inventor inhabited.

Edison's face unexpectedly twisted with a silly grin. "How about I wrap up this session with one of my favorites." Swinging his arms and marching in place, he began singing, "I'm a Yankee Doodle Dandy! A Yankee Doodle, do or die…"

As Sarah listened, she thought *she* would die. Edison's rendition was god-awful, yet Sarah politely giggled and cheered, "Bravo!" as Cutting translated the remainder of her dialogue. "This has been a great occasion on all accounts, but unfortunately I must catch a train to Boston. Thank you, Mr. Edison, for this rare opportunity to peek into the future."

Edison graciously bowed. "It has been my pleasure. And I'm pleased that your voice shall be the first ever recorded in history to recite those precious lines. Well, Madame, best wishes in Boston. As for me, I must get back to my bulbs. Farewell, my lady!"

As Sarah turned and commenced to exit, she softly uttered, *"Adieu,"* followed once again by, *"Mai l'éclat léger!"*

Cutting promptly escorted Sarah to her carriage, while Edison contemplatively stood by the breezy doorway. With a crack of the whip, the horses bucked as warm vapor shot out their nostrils into the cold November air. Obediently they trotted forward, as Sarah's carriage hobbled away over the cobblestoned street. Cutting turned and walked slowly back under the darkening sky, poorly lit by a string of malodorous gas lamps.

Edison's curiosity, however, could no longer be bridled. "Robert! What in tarnation was that *Mai lee* thing she uttered?"

Cutting smiled. "Ah, you mean *Mai l'éclat léger*. That means 'May the light shine!'"

❄ ❄ ❄

The famous diva had in fact visited Edison at Menlo Park. Despite the fictional dialogue, laced with authentic quotes by Edison, it wasn't long before Edison not only illuminated New York City, but the entire nation, as well as parts of Europe. His dispute with Swan over their incandescent bulb was resolved in England by a merger that formed the Ediswan Company. Edison effectively promoted his new invention as not only being more cost effective than the malodorous gas lamps, but even slighted the outdated and dangerous device by stating, "Gas was a light for the dark ages."

Railroad tycoon John Pierpont Morgan perceptively recognized the lucrative future of electricity and became Edison's primary financier. J.P. Morgan invested in many peripheral industries, and by routinely holding a majority of shares, he omnipotently power-managed each of them. This finally enabled Edison to implement his modern marvel, and at an accelerated rate. One of his first feats was to retrofit Morgan's New York office with electric lighting. Other affluent families, such as the Vanderbilts, utilized Edison to electrify their estates, while business offices and factories soon followed. Eventually, in 1881, the city of New York commissioned Edison to install lampposts and wiring throughout the city. In time, subsequent mergers allowed Edison's lighting system to spread across the nation, illuminating streets and homes, while his European satellite followed suit. Edison was effectively snuffing out the archaic age of gas lamps.

However, Edison's eventual success was not void of obstacles. One of Edison's early roadblocks was how to solve the immense power source that his electrical network required. Batteries were the only known source of electricity during his pioneering days and they couldn't sustain the vast network Edison envisioned.

Alessandro Volta had made the astounding invention of the battery over a century earlier in 1799. By first devising the electrophorus in 1775, Volta managed to produce static electricity. However, static discharges yielded nothing useful. Volta then discovered that when certain metals and chemicals encountered one another, they produced electricity. For the first time, man could not only create, but also harness the raw power of nature, which previously merely fascinated them. This opened a huge doorway to electrical research and experimentation. His revolutionary invention attracted the attention of the famous emperor, Napoleon Bonaparte, who presented Volta with a cash award and even minted gold coins in his honor. The term *volt* was applied to the electro current in 1881, which is still used today, thus commemorating his electrifying achievement.

Yet, it was only after witnessing the dynamo generator, built by William Wallace, that the key to successfully lighting large networks dawned upon Edison. It was Edison's improvements to this generator that finally enabled him to power his broad network with a modicum of stability.

At the outbreak of WWI, Edison was invited to Washington DC, and protected by the Secret Service, where he developed over forty inventions for the navy. Some of these inventions were as follows: fitting naval searchlights with rapid-action Venetian-blinds to send visual Morse Code; devising a chemical, soda-based fire extinguisher that stripped fire of its oxygen; developing a gyro-like platform for mounted guns to correct aim in rolling seas; modifying periscopes to enhance clarity; devising underwater parachute-like bags that, when deployed, could more quickly turn or slow down a ship.

Henry Ford

Edison then devoted much time to developing a new and more cost-efficient rubber that aided Henry Ford's rising automotive needs. The post-WWI years had marked a tremendous shift in innovation. One that even Edison was growing uncomfortable with. The new age made clear how trains confined to tracks were yielding to automobiles on an open road, or how Bell's telephone, confined by wire, was yielding to Marconi's radio that was wireless and boundless.

Edison strongly opposed radio, in particular, as it rivaled his interests in the telephonic, telegraphic, and phonographic industries. He even declared it a "fad" that wouldn't last. However, it later became President Franklin Roosevelt's favorite medium, as his fireside chats were broadcast into American homes via invisible wireless signals. A new rapidly progressive world had emerged, one that even Edison was finding hard to keep pace with.

Edison's impressive list of inventions includes: the electrical vote recorder; universal stock ticker; electrical fuses, sockets and regulation meters required for the massive electrical network; the fluorescent lamp; the nickel-iron-alkaline storage battery; the miner's helmet with safety light;

as well as over forty naval innovations and many others. Last, and certainly not least, is Edison's patent of the motion picture camera. This was actually developed by Thomas Armat and Charles Jenkins, from whom Edison bought the rights, and this device would likewise have an incalculable effect on modern culture.

As a young boy born in Ohio, Thomas' family soon moved to Michigan where his schooling would soon prove brief. After only three months, Edison's humiliated teacher pronounced him incapable of focusing or learning. Thomas was homeschooled by his mother, who prompted his appetite for reading. As such, Edison soon became a voracious reader.

However, by age twelve, it was evident that Edison already had profound hearing loss, which certainly accounts for his learning debacle at school. Edison's hearing progressively deteriorated. Finding it an asset to close out the outside world to better focus on his experiments, Edison later denied pleas from deaf people that begged him to develop a hearing aid.

In 1837, the young Edison became infatuated with Samuel F. B. Morse's telegraph. By the end of the Civil War, telegraph cables stretched across America from San Francisco to Washington DC. Edison quickly became a telegrapher and relocated several times, each time gaining ground in the new industry. Eventually, the innovative youngster was given corporate backing to develop a new and faster stock ticker.

By 1876, Alexander Graham Bell had invented the telephone, and for the next two years, Edison worked on perfecting his speaking telegraph. He even perfected Bell's telephone by adding two carbon buttons formed out of kerosene lampblack. This finally made the device consumer-ready. However, during these years of experimentation, the partially deaf inventor needed to place a metal plate between his teeth that was connected to a sounding apparatus in order to hear.

Despite his stubbornness, Edison often strived to find solutions to overcome adversity. During his experimentation with hearing aids Edison realized that if he could record these signals, he could then possibly reproduce and play back the sound. This endeavor would inevitably give birth to Edison's phonograph.

However, Edison's primary focus was on lighting, and by initially electrifying New York City, his enterprise soon expanded nationwide and caught the world's attention. And with J.P. Morgan's shrewd and powerful financial backing Edison was able to form a monopoly in the electrical consumption industry. By the early 1880s, Edison had his lab in Menlo Park, New Jersey, and power plants in New York City as well as in Europe. But, being the master puppeteer, J.P. Morgan would change all that in the future.

NIKOLA TESLA: *Overshadowed Genius*

In 1884, Edison was introduced to Nikola Tesla, a Croatian-born Serbian immigrant seeking work. Tesla was a young wizard in his own right who worked as a troubleshooter for Edison's power plants in France and Germany. In fact, Tesla first witnessed Edison's Dynamo DC electric generator in his college class at the Polytechnic Institute in Austria. Fortunately for Tesla, Edison had just received a distress call regarding broken dynamos aboard a ship he had recently outfitted. Tesla was employed on the spot to remedy the electrical malfunction, which he did at lightning speed.

Tesla was instantly hired and diligently aided Edison in the struggle to invent generators powerful enough to transmit current over a broad network. Tesla was a workaholic and put in fifteen to seventeen hours a day, prompting Edison to remark, "I have had many hardworking assistants, but you take the cake!" However, a recurring dispute kept erupting as Tesla kept suggesting his

AC (alternating current), which he claimed was superior. Edison wasn't interested; he was deeply invested with labor and patents on his existing DC (direct current) system. In essence, Edison now viewed Tesla as a nuisance, while Tesla grew more and more frustrated.

Tesla was a rare and versatile genius. Yet even Tesla's amazing discoveries were in small part indebted to previous patents by other inventors. His alternating current motor was a modification of the works that several scientists developed, yet most prominent was Elihu Thomson, who had already designed and operated motors on the AC system. Thomson was a prolific inventor, and secured more patents than even Tesla. Thomson had also established his own electric company when he partnered with a friend to form the Thomson-Houston Company.

However, hovering above all these electrical wizards was a hawkish titan, who carefully eyed up the unsuspecting Thomson, and this, once again, was J.P. Morgan. Morgan's typical cutthroat practice was to establish rival companies, only to undercut prices, which forced his rivals to renegotiate contracts and company shares, allowing Morgan to consume a fifty-one percent majority holding. Morgan had appointed Charles Coffin in charge of leading this devious capitalistic assault. Eventually, Thomson was forced to merge with Edison Electric to form a new powerhouse company, whereby Morgan effectively erased both inventors' names from the nameplate, thus becoming General Electric.

Morgan now fully controlled his lilliputian subjects, and quite appropriately, his appointee had the perfect name, for as far as name recognition went, Charles had nailed both Thomson and Edison's coffins shut.

However, before the merger, Tesla had secured many new patents for the Edison Company, until irreconcilable differences peaked. Tesla finally had enough and quit. This was due to personal, as well as serious financial conflicts with Edison. Although both men were geniuses, they were polar opposites. Tesla was academically educated, quiet, and extremely fastidious, while Edison was self-educated, often brusque in manner, and unkempt. Tesla even mocked the older genius for being appallingly disorganized. However, beyond inventive genius, Edison also possessed an intuitive business acumen, which Tesla lacked. This would plague Tesla for the rest of his long and inventively fruitful life. Nevertheless, Tesla then found employment with Edison's rival.

GEORGE WESTINGHOUSE was a dynamic force in his own right, and his investment in AC motors and transformers, created by William Stanley Jr., persuaded him to challenge Edison's DC system. Westinghouse had previously developed the first commercial AC system, consisting of thirty plants in Buffalo, New York in November of 1886. Therefore, when Westinghouse heard of Tesla's breakthroughs and patents, which included polyphase AC motors, transformers, and all the accessories necessary to run a new and infinitely far superior AC system, Westinghouse leapt at the opportunity to secure Tesla.

George Westinghouse

Yet even Westinghouse was caught in the snare of dealing with J.P. Morgan and his prized wizard, Edison. Westinghouse was a man of strong principles, and a staunch advocate for progress. Not just financial progress, but scientific progress. This meant that even if an existing and expensive system was already in place, it would be prudent, and in everyone's best interest, to change it if a superior system presented itself. This was not always true with Edison, and especially not with the moneyman, Morgan, whose prime concern was bottom-line profits.

Interestingly, Mark Twain summed up this era of robber barons rather nicely when he said their credo was, "Get money. Get it quickly. Get it in abundance. Get it dishonestly, if you can, honestly, if you must."

Westinghouse, however, was a different breed, for he knew that AC was superior. And with the advent of Tesla's patents, which distinctly demonstrated that AC was more advanced, Westinghouse, like David, stood up to the Goliaths that monopolized the industry. This duel became known as the "War of the Currents".

Yet while Westinghouse unveiled his slingshot of truth and progress, Edison unsheathed his sword of underhanded greed and suppression. Edison's subordinates engaged in many smear tactics that today would be crimes. They had dogs, cats, and even an elephant electrocuted in public using the high voltage of AC as a demonstration of the system's many dangers, while labeling the dead victims as being "Westinghoused". They even took this to an unprecedented level when Sing Sing Prison decided to make a first in history by electrocuting the criminal William Kemmler. The executioner's stage was set and the switch thrown, yet the Edison technicians miscalculated the voltage required, since they had previously killed only small animals. Kemmler would suffer a torturous death, as the electrical jolt had to be repeated to terminate his quivering nerves. Westinghouse was mortified. However, this spurred respected scientists to rally to Westinghouse's side, whereby they published proven statistics that soundly countered the unfounded hype.

Edison, however, was wielding a double-edged sword. For on one side, although he originally refused AC (perhaps out of jealousy), as an inventor he had to have known that AC was a superior technology, one he unfortunately did not invent or legally possess. On the other side, Edison also had to contend with the fiscal-minded J.P. Morgan, who inevitably called all the shots. As the man who pulled all the strings and controlled Edison's purse and fate, Morgan would not jeopardize his profits by overhauling an entire system just to accommodate the public. Edison may have been the brilliant puppet, but Morgan was the puppet master.

However, while Westinghouse battled these titans, his market share dropped, and he soon found himself in a crisis. Westinghouse was instructed by his financial advisors to repair the gaping hole that was sinking his ship. The hole happened to be the over-generous royalty he had agreed to pay Tesla for his AC polyphase system. The fiscal analysis was clear; if the leaking fissure persisted the Westinghouse flagship would surely sink. Being an inventor himself, Westinghouse believed in generous royalties for scientific ingenuity. As such, he detested the admiral's call to duty, which forced him to order his first mate to either sacrifice his share of the treasure, or watch the entire ship sink. Therefore, with heavy heart, Westinghouse approached Tesla and relayed the ultimatum, "*Your* decision determines the fate of the Westinghouse Company."

Tesla paused, then questioned Westinghouse about his loyalty to the AC System. Westinghouse professed his dream and determination in succinct terms, "It was my efforts to make it available to the world that brought about the present difficulty. But, I intend to continue, no matter what happens, with my original plans to put the country on an alternating-current basis."

Tesla was a diehard scientist; the benefits of his endeavors for society came before his own personal gain. Moreover, he knew that if he was cast out to sea there were no other flagships to climb aboard. His patents for his new AC polyphase system would sink with him, while the resolute Westinghouse would rise and establish another fleet to continue the assault, even with a whole new crew if necessary. Evidently, Tesla realized the sincerity and goodwill of the man before him, and conceded. Many years later, Tesla would recollect how Westinghouse was the only man in the struggle who was a true friend, a genuine man of honor, and a true benefactor of progress. Likewise, Tesla realized that Westinghouse supported him and his dazzling invention with his own hide, and desperately needed a sacrificial compromise to stay afloat. Tesla would receive a flat fee of $216,600 for his AC patents, and Westinghouse remained in business.

Under the revised contract, Tesla was required to move to Westinghouse's Pittsburgh plant to conduct the implementation and development. However, Tesla soon became embroiled in intense arguments with the plant's engineers who wished to maintain standard practices. Tesla, meanwhile, endured as best he could. Upon completing his consulting, Tesla decided he had had enough, and established his own lab in New York City with money he had saved. This is when Tesla invented the Tesla coil, which transformed high voltage down to safe levels for use in appliances. He also began research on radio transmission.

While Tesla was consumed in his own world of research and invention, Westinghouse phoned him from Pittsburgh. Westinghouse was ecstatic; he had won the contract for powering the upcoming World's Fair in Chicago. This event was scheduled to celebrate the 400th anniversary of Columbus' discovery, and was projected to attract millions worldwide. They would finally have their chance to show the world the awesome power of AC. Moreover, they would also set an historic benchmark by being the first to use AC current to power a World's Fair. However, not only would the eyes of the world be focused on the event (which would feature exciting new inventions by Edison, grand classical architecture and, of course, their new AC system), but the country was in a slump with unemployment, bankruptcies, and foreclosures, as Grover Cleveland took office for a second term. Therefore, the country also needed a grand spectacle to boost morale and incite new markets of interest and development. It was January of 1893, and they only had four months to complete the huge task. Henceforth, Tesla had to drop everything he was laboring on in New York to make the fair a success.

The Chicago World's Fair (Columbian Exposition) opened on May 1 and exceeded expectations in all spheres. By September, over 25 million people attended, as new fangled wonders of all kinds were on display, including the 250-foot rotating wheel with seats designed by Mr. George Ferris. This also allowed Westinghouse to display his own contributions to the AC system, which included transformers that could convert AC to DC, making it universally adaptable to preexisting appliances or even trolleys. Westinghouse and Tesla scored a huge success, and by October of 1893, Westinghouse had already received a call for their next big project. He was awarded the contract to build the first two generators that would harness the power of Niagara Falls.

As a young boy, Tesla had been fascinated by watermills and turbines, and had even seen a photo of the mighty Niagara Falls in one of his father's books. The sheer size of the falls, and thoughts of how to harness its power, captivated Tesla. Now he had the chance and expertise to tackle his childhood dream. With the superior AC System perfected by Tesla, and the perseverance and sound business acumen of Westinghouse, Niagara Falls became a milestone in electrical engineering. The initial facility produced a staggering 150,000 horsepower of electricity, and with General Electric being awarded the task of installing the power lines as a fair contractual compromise, the city of Buffalo, New York was set ablaze with current. The Westinghouse/Tesla success at this facility made clear that AC was, in fact, a superior solution, and in the years that followed, it effectively replaced Edison's DC system.

Edison had previously strung wires haphazardly across cities using his DC network, yet as the years passed, the harsh reality of this system's inherent flaws mounted and became painfully evident. Fires were prevalent and DC generators often required repairs. The DC system could only transmit electricity short distances, and only allowed for a single voltage. Hence, although being sufficient for light bulbs, since bulbs all drew an equal amount of current, appliances such as the new refrigerators and fans being invented, required more voltage, thus confirming that DC was obsolete. In contrast, the AC method, developed initially by others, yet perfected by Tesla, effectively allowed for this variance. However, despite AC's luminous success, and the colossal impact it would have on all electrical systems across the globe, Tesla remained an overshadowed genius.

Nikola Tesla maintained a small circle of friends, but was predominantly a loner, as many creative talents are, and was erroneously described by some as insane or a mad scientist. This image was further enhanced by his invention of the Magnifying Transmitter in the late 1890s, which produced huge, flaring arcs of electricity 20 to 30 feet long. This wildly charged apparatus became synonymous with the mad scientist, as similar mock devices were used in Hollywood for the early Frankenstein films. However, the real basis for these people's assessments was his odd behaviors. Tesla was known to circle a building three times before entering, demanded that eighteen clean linen napkins be neatly folded at each and every meal, and he required a similar amount of towels for each and every bath. Tesla's servant also recorded other repetitious oddities that promulgated the rumors. However, modern analysis of Tesla's condition indicates that he had OCD, obsessive-compulsive-disorder. This nagging affliction, however, did not have an effect on Tesla's lucidity or inventiveness, which remained extremely active.

Tesla was a close friend of Mark Twain for many years. The photograph on left captures Twain in Tesla's lab, standing near one of Tesla's illuminated spheres. The spheres where illuminated by an ambient oscillator nearby, making them completely wireless, and could be held or even moved freely around the room. Tesla also demonstrated to Twain and an English journalist, Chauncey McGovern, his red ball of flames. Tesla snapped his fingers, and this odd phenomenon (without a glass tube or container, or an apparent power source) appeared in his hand. He then placed this glowing red ball of flames on his clothes, in his hair, and even on his bewildered spectators' laps, all without the slightest burn or injury. Tesla was an astounding scientist with a plethora of bold ideas that, unfortunately, weren't brought to fruition by investors and, even more unfortunately, were never fully documented by Tesla. As such, a multitude of intriguing experiments died with their luminous master.

Tesla's earlier battle with Edison over the AC/DC systems caused both men to become more embittered as the years progressed. When the nomination for the Nobel Prize in 1915 was rumored to include both Edison and Tesla sharing the honor, each inventor rose in heated opposition, swearing never to share the award. It's ironic that neither would receive this prestigious award, yet the inventiveness of both men helped immeasurably in shaping a nation, a nation positioning itself to be a world leader.

The turn of the century saw many new inventions, and the Industrial Revolution, with its earlier roots in England, now became more pronounced on American soil. In fact, this trend was well charted; in the 1870s, America produced about 23 percent of the world's manufacturing output, and by 1929, it was producing over 42 percent. Meanwhile, England produced 32 percent in the 1870s, which dropped down to 9.5 percent by 1929.

Henry Ford's automated production line ushered in advances that proved crucial to both World Wars, and had an incalculable impact on all modern manufacturing. Like Edison, Henry Ford had no formal education yet his contribution to the war effort, American society, and the world of manufacturing was beyond colossal. Edison's phonograph, movie camera, and the original concept and installation of an electrical network that powered lights and small appliances indelibly changed the world. His DC System proved to be defective, but it was Edison who first conceived and implemented an electrical system well before Tesla perfected it with AC. Tesla and Westinghouse, on the other hand, made this system what it is today; extremely adaptable, electrically safe, cost effective, and resoundingly effective and universal.

The beginning of the twentieth century had closed its doors on the listless nineteenth century of gas and wicks, thus opening its doors to the lightning-fast world of electricity and light. This shocking transformation was largely due to Edison's pioneering role, while the additional critical genius of Tesla and the business acumen of Morgan and Westinghouse completed the circuit.

LUDINGTON & ARMISTEAD:
Unsung Heroes

Sybil Ludington's Midnight Ride

It was April 26, 1777, almost two years to the day that the first mysterious shot launched the Revolutionary War in Lexington, and the battle still raged. The Continental Army, under General George Washington's command, had suffered a devastating blow only six months earlier when the British won a series of battles, forcing Washington to abandon Manhattan, Long Island, and its crucial New York harbor.

Colonel Henry Ludington, who had served as George Washington's aide during the humiliating retreat at White Plains, was now in command of the 7th Dutchess County Militia, based out of his house in Kent, New York, some seventy-five miles north of Manhattan.

April 26 was a wet and stormy night, and Henry's four-hundred-man regiment were all home on furlough, having recently completed a tour of duty. Happy for the reprieve, the colonel lit his pipe as he sat by the hearth with two aides and a sergeant in his meager farmhouse. While discussing their farming and milling trades and possible war initiatives, a hammering blow rattled the door!

Henry glanced at his sixteen-year-old daughter, Sybil. She was the eldest of his twelve children, and intently listening to their conversation, rather than helping her mother prepare dinner. "Get that, honey, will you!" Henry instructed.

As the door continued to rattle with a flurry of anxious blows, Sybil turned the iron latch and opened the door. Barging in was a young messenger, his hair wet and plastered to his head and his clothes, sopping wet.

As driving rain splattered the threshold, Sybil quickly closed the door.

"Colonel Ludington!" the twenty-year-old gushed. "I come from Danbury...to alert you!" he exclaimed as he gasped for air.

The Colonel stood up. "Alert me to what, son. Go on!"

Swallowing hard and catching his breath, he replied, "The British landed on the shores of Fairfield, Connecticut yesterday...with twenty transports and six warships. Major General Tryon and two thousand redcoats are sacking Danbury right now as we speak! Its all ablaze, Sir!"

Henry flinched as he nearly dropped his pipe. He recalled how William Tryon—former governor of New York, and now major general—had conspired to kidnap General George Washington and assassinate his chief officers. The deadly plot had failed, but Tryon's machinations had only escalated during the war. He was notorious for savage brutality, and allowing his thugs to marauder and even rape when the impulse struck them. Moreover, Tryon knew that

British General Howe had placed a 300 English guineas reward on Henry's head, dead or alive, and that added more fuel to Tryon's death march.

Yet Henry's own troubles were of little concern. That Danbury was in flames, and their main food supplies and munitions being destroyed demanded an immediate response. The Continental Army had recently moved everything from Peekskill to Danbury, thinking it would be safer, but now all seemed lost.

Henry's face tensed up as he blurted, "Damn them! Tryon and his scoundrels are destroying our food depot. How in hell did they find out!?" Henry's face twitched. "Good Lord, and Danbury is poorly manned."

As thunder clapped and rain pelted the windows, Henry's aides and the sergeant nervously leapt to their feet, as one aide bellowed, "My God! What are we to do, Colonel? Those stores hold all of our beef, pork, wheat, and several cases of wine and rum. And our regiment is on furlough, not even organized."

Before Henry could answer, the other aide added, "Never mind not organized, they're not even in our midst, scattered all about the countryside and beyond."

The sergeant nervously blinked and added, "And Danbury is some twenty miles from here, as well. How in God's name can we ever intercede?"

Henry waved his hand. "Easy boys, let's not lose our heads." Furiously, he scratched his chin, having all to do to maintain a sense of calm amid his men. As he paced the small living room, the messenger wiped his wet face and said, "If I may, Colonel, my commander, Colonel Cooke, told me that General Benedict Arnold will be receiving word of this, as well. Perhaps he can help us."

Henry turned his gaze toward the gangly lad, and replied, "General Arnold is situated in New Haven, is he not?"

The messenger nodded.

"Jesus!" Henry blurted. "That's a good thirty-five miles from Danbury, as well." A surge of nervous adrenaline moistened Henry's undergarments, as he rubbed his temple, thinking. As Sybil gazed at her father intently, Henry's eyes calculatingly rolled, as he added, "Hmm, Danbury sits right between us and Arnold, yet at quite some distance."

Henry's aide chimed in, "But General Arnold has his troops *at* his side, Colonel. *W-we do not!"* he added with a nervous crack in his voice.

"Yes, yes, I know!" Henry chided. "But if we can muster our troops expeditiously, we can both ambush General Tryon; a pincer maneuver that could teach these damned Brits just who the hell they're dealing with."

The sergeant swallowed hard. "But 'expeditiously' *is* the problem, Colonel. We cannot afford to waste a single man to round up all of our scattered patriots, as we need to gather our gear first, and then get rolling towards Danbury as soon as possible."

Henry waved his hand in a patting motion. "I know, I know," he said, as he looked out the window at the driving rain. "And this damned weather is of no help, either."

"I'll go!" a voice rang out.

All the men gazed around, trying to locate the source of the unexpected voice, when their eyes fell upon the culprit. It was young Sybil!

As the men shook their heads with patronizing smirks, Henry gazed at his daughter and replied sternly, "This is no joking matter, Sybil!"

Sybil stepped boldly forward, now standing inches away from her father, as she gazed up into his slate-blue eyes. "I can do this, Pa. I can. And you know it!"

Henry felt a wave of embarrassment wash over him. He never expected to be challenged like this, especially in front of his men. If he had a sixteen year old son, fine, but a *young girl!?*

The sergeant hastily buttoned up his jacket, as he gazed at his commander. "Excuse me, Sir, but we really have no time for this. What are we going to do?"

Henry looked at the young messenger. "Are you available to make the ride, son?"

The messenger shook his head. "I apologize, Sir, although I *am* available, I live in Connecticut and don't know these parts at all. God knows how I made it here. Besides, Danbury is under siege, they need every hand available."

Henry stood momentarily mute, then turned toward his impatient sergeant. "Sybil will make the ride."

As the aides' eyes bulged, the sergeant gasped. "You can't be serious, Colonel!?"

"I'm dead serious, Sergeant! My daughter is indeed one of the best riders in Dutchess County."

The sergeant huffed, as his hands clenched with frustration. "With all due respect, Colonel, we *cannot* place such a critical demand as this upon a young girl. Men's lives are at stake, not only in Danbury, but in this whole darn revolt of ours, which, as you know, we suffered a brutal shellacking only several months ago with Washington's devastating losses!"

Henry stepped boldly in front of the sergeant. "Listen, Sergeant," he said with commanding gravity, "Washington may have lost New York, but his crossing of the Delaware in the freezing snow and ice to capture Trenton will go down as one of the most strategically daring and courageous attacks in world history. It is only through such unconventional thinking and unusual bravery that we can ever hope to succeed against the superior might of Britain."

As Henry looked deep into his subdued sergeant's eyes, the young messenger cleared his throat and interrupted, "Excuse me, sirs, but Colonel Cooke ordered me to return at once."

Henry pivoted about. "Of course. Tell him we *will* be in Danbury, come hell or high water! You're dismissed." Turning back toward his daughter, he added with urgency, "Saddle up, Sybil! You must leave at once." He gazed at the clock; it was 9:00 PM. Turning toward his aide, he added, "Bring me the local map, Patrick, quickly!"

As Patrick issued the map, Henry pointed to all the key villages that Sybil had to alert. As she analyzed the familiar map, the young messenger bolted out the door, his muddy boots leaving a trail of sloppy footprints in his wake.

Sybil clutched her blue woolen overcoat and buttoned it up, as her father grasped her shoulders firmly. "Now, Sybil, are you sure you can handle this? This ride will be nearly forty miles, more than twice what Paul Revere had been tasked with."

Sybil smiled, and with a firm nod, she said, "Of course, Papa. But where Mr. Revere never succeeded in making it to Concord, I guarantee that I will alert all of your men, from those down in Mahopac all the way up to Stormville."

Henry chuckled. "You've always been a feisty lass, Sybil." His face grew tense with concern. "But by God's grace, please make it back safely. The area is teaming with British soldiers and even treacherous Tories, who would turn you in for a chicken egg. Do you hear me?" As Sybil nodded, Henry hugged his daughter with a burning passion, which hitherto, he had never expressed before. The thought of losing her was unthinkable. He gazed into her young, perky eyes, which radiated determination and excitement, recalling his own enthusiasm and heroism when he, as a young lad, had fought in the French and Indian War.

Being the oldest child, Sybil not only pitched in as an auxiliary parent, taking care of her younger sisters and brothers, but also deftly handled an assortment of tasks, from sewing and knitting to making soap and candles. Being a bit of a tomboy, Sybil had also taken it upon herself to train her yearling, a strong gelding named Star.

Henry kissed his precious daughter firmly on the forehead and spun her about. As he escorted her to the door, the sergeant and aides scurried to prepare for battle. Sybil exited the house and ran through the rain to the stable. Unhitching her trusty brown gelding—that was named Star due to the white-shaped patch on its forehead—Sybil saddled him up and walked him to the stable door. She then picked up a sturdy branch and removed all the leaves, per her father's instructions. It would serve multiple purposes. Whipping the ground several times to test its resilience, she then hopped on Star, clutched the reins in one hand, and slapped his hefty rear with the stick.

Dashing into the driving rain, Sybil galloped through a labyrinth of trees and open fields, over the mountains and down through the soggy valleys, as thunderclouds choked the night sky.

As she rode, she contemplated how Paul Revere had the good fortune of traversing a fairly manicured terrain, while she was beleaguered by a mountainous wilderness. Adding to her woes was the god-awful weather.

As the deluge relentlessly smacked the leaves and grass, while thunder roared in the distance, Sybil rode through village after village, knocking on doors with her stick and alerting all to the advancing British. Local farmers, cobblers, and blacksmiths rallied their families, preparing for the potential onslaught, while Ludington's militiamen grabbed their muskets and saddled up.

On her way down to Mahopac, Sybil struggled to recognize familiar landmarks, as the pitch black of night coupled with heavy rainfall disoriented her, not to mention how many townsfolk had already gone to bed, leaving their houses as black as the night. After successfully navigating her way to Mahopac, Sybil then turned and headed north, riding along the shoreline of several lakes toward Carmel. Upon her arrival, she trotted through the streets, sounding the alarm. "The British are burning Danbury, meet at Ludington's!"

Townsfolk stepped out of their candlelit dwellings, some still in their pajamas and holding lanterns, to hear her call, while the militiamen quickly began gearing up. The bells of Carmel's church began pealing; amplifying the alarm, as rain mercilessly pelted the belfry.

One young man called out, "Would you mind if I join you? I hear there are plenty of Tories about these parts, not to mention Skinners."

Sybil was well aware of the dangers, including the dreaded Skinners; outlaws without allegiances to any side and without scruples of any kind. She pointed with her stick to the east. "It's best if we split up. Head eastward, quickly! I'm heading to Stormville."

The volunteer nodded and mounted his horse, while Sybil slapped Star's rear and dashed northward.

As she galloped through a dark wooded path, she spotted a blurry silhouette up ahead. Anxiously, she tried to blink the rain out of her eyes. As the black vision began to materialize, she realized it was a highwayman, waving for her to stop. As she approached, the man stepped in front of her horse and spread his arms out wide, a musket in one hand.

"Halt!" he barked. "My danged horse abandoned me. Dumb mule hightailed it while I was relieving myself in the bushes." He lowered his hands. "I need a ride home, gal."

Sybil steadied Star, who was getting anxious, and she replied politely, "I'm sorry, sir, but I have an important mission to accomplish. My father is Colonel Ludington, and I must..."

"You *must* take me home, girl!" the man spat, his face contorting with irritation. "And I mean *quickly!"* With an agitated huff, the man raised his musket. "Now you be a good little girl and get down from that horse." With eyes glowing with venom, he barked, "NOW!"

Sybil quaked in her soggy boots, her nerves now tingling with pinching waves of adrenaline. "Y-yes, sir," she stammered.

As she maneuvered Star closer, the man cocked his musket. "And no funny stuff, missy!"

"Of c-course not, sir," she replied respectfully, trying to maintain her calm. Instantaneously, Sybil snapped her stick, slapping the weapon out of his hands! With a firm kick of her heels, Star bolted forward, nearly knocking the man to the ground, as they galloped into the night rain. As she sped away, Sybil's mind flashed back to her father; thanking him for imparting the many uses of a good stick, and his rule to never dismount her horse for a stranger.

Making her way to Stormville, Sybil sounded the alert and then made a hasty beeline back home. Arriving at dawn, Sybil was greeted by her anxious father and family, who all hugged. Better yet, the majority of minutemen were already present and accounted for. The joyful reunion, however, was brief, for the real battle was yet to begin.

Colonel Ludington swiftly led his men across state lines into neighboring Connecticut, and headed south to Danbury. Unfortunately, they arrived too late, as Tryon and his men had burned their storage facilities and several homes, being that upon entering town they had marked houses owned by loyalists with chalk, while those that were unmarked were homes of rebel patriots, which were duly burned. Ludington was livid!

Yet despite the humiliation that all their foodstuffs were gone, there was one small bonus. The redcoats had drank all their rum and had partied and pilfered all night long. As such, their retreat southward toward Ridgefield would make them easy pickings. And as sure as the ease of killing drunken, sitting ducks, the British, despite having three-times as many men, were brutally badgered their entire journey south. Ludington's forces, supplemented by Continental troops from the east, engaged in guerilla tactics and forced the British back to the shores of Long Island Sound. Despite Tryon's victory at Danbury, which entailed arson, pillage, and exacting a sizeable death toll, the British Army would never again make expeditionary maneuvers through the state of Connecticut.

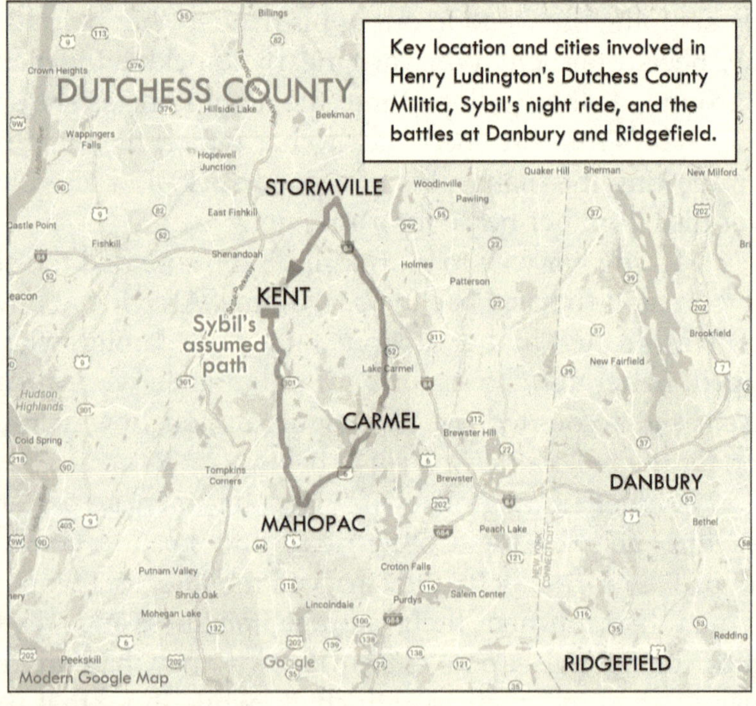

While the majority of this tale is factual, the part dealing with Sybil's ride has been told over many years with limited primary sources and in various versions. It is undisputable, however, that Sybil made the forty-mile ride amid a torrential thunderstorm, and successfully alerted her father's men to arms. Some of the varying details, such as who exactly was home when the messenger arrived, the tolling of church bells, the man who asked to assist her, and the highwayman who she averted, made no clear indication as to what exactly transpired and artistic license has been used to embellish these particular events.

Even Sybil's name has been changed over the years, for she herself had spelled her name "Sebal" on her Revolutionary War pension application.

Nevertheless, Sybil was congratulated not only by her family and all those in Dutchess County, but also by General George Washington. Even Alexander Hamilton wrote to her father, stating "I congratulate you on the Danbury expedition. The stores destroyed have been purchased at a pretty high price to the enemy."

Therefore, despite the minor discrepancies in fine details, Sybil's night ride amid darkness and driving rain, which was in fact twice as long and arduous as Paul Revere's, makes this sixteen-year-old girl's trek a highly laudable piece of early American heroism; one that all men, and especially women, can be most proud.

James Armistead Lafayette

James was born approximately in 1748, in New Kent County, Virginia. The exact date of his birth and name, other than James, are not known. He was later referred to as James Armistead, James Lafayette, and James Armistead Lafayette, for reasons that will become apparent.

James was the slave of William Armistead, hence taking on the surname of his master. During the Revolutionary War William Armistead had taken on the role of state commissary of military supplies, and was stationed in Richmond, Virginia. At his side was his slave servant,

James, who asked his master a rather shocking question; namely, could he join the war effort against the British?

Certainly the Patriots had suffered many defeats and setbacks since the war's beginning and could use any help offered, yet James' request was atypical in that the British had cleverly offered colonial slaves their freedom if they abandoned their masters and joined the British. Moreover, General Washington had waivered on the topic of allowing black men (freedmen or slaves) to join the Continental Army. The thought of arming blacks, especially slaves, with muskets and weapons had gripped many slave owners with fear of rebellion, and Washington agreed. However, once Washington heard of the British offer, he changed his decision. Even though, blacks had no guarantee of achieving their freedom afterwards, so James' request to volunteer was perhaps one born of an innate love for his homeland, or he might have viewed the Patriots as the lesser of two evils.

Nevertheless, James was duly put into the service of the French military officer Marquis de Lafayette. Lafayette had previously served the Patriots by enduring a deadly frigid winter at Valley Forge along with General Washington, so his bravery and commitment to the cause of rebellion for independence was highly laudable by any standards. Recently, however, he had been asked by Washington to move his forces to Virginia in response to the

Marquis de Lafayette

threat posed by Generals Arnold and Phillips. Moreover, he was instructed to gather intelligence, which had proved to be one of General Washington's most treasured resources to fight the superior might of the British.

As such, Lafayette welcomed James Armistead into the fold. His first task was to infiltrate the camp of the once-honored-now-loathed General Benedict Arnold. James succeeded in doing so and fed Lafayette information that led to the successful ambush of Arnold's camp, which almost offered the prize of capturing the traitorous general himself.

General Charles Cornwallis

James was given the second and more critical task of gathering intelligence from British General Charles Cornwallis. Cornwallis had intrepidly marched his troops from the Carolinas up to Virginia, and set Richmond ablaze. That his 7,200 troops outnumbered Lafayette's 3,200 troops accentuated the dire need to acquire critical intelligence.

As such, in July of 1781, James managed to infiltrate Cornwallis' camp and posed as a waiter. That James was a black man added to his cover, as the British were confident that no slave would forfeit their freedom to be a spy.

Therefore, as James cordially served his masters, while they discussed strategies and key tactical locations, he mentally recorded every detail. This included the amount of British ships in the Hampton Roads area and near Yorktown. James also smuggled papers and overheard Cornwallis say that he intended to remain in Yorktown longer than anticipated.

Utilizing James' highly prized information, Lafayette's smaller forces had the critical element of surprise on their side, and now also knew where Cornwallis was stationed. Coordinating a multi-pronged attack with General Washington, Lafayette managed to direct the French navy into Chesapeake Bay to blockade the York River. Meanwhile, Washington marched his troops south to Williamsburg to join Lafayette.

By October 19, 1781, Washington and Lafayette's forces prevailed, with the aid of Alexander Hamilton, Lt. Col. John Laurens and French commander Marquis de Noailles. Despite General Cornwallis' refusal to meet General Washington for the official surrender, his capitulation yielded for the Patriots over 7,000 surrendered British troops and over 800 British sailors.

Surrender of British General Cornwallis

The intelligence gathered by James proved highly valuable, and Lafayette made it a point to inform Washington about a "Correspondant of Mine Servant to Lord Cornwallis," that attained such information.

Washington is said to have congratulated James. And while General Cornwallis refused to meet with Washington, he did, however, meet with Marquis de Lafayette. Evidently, Cornwallis viewed Lafayette as a noble officer of a true and regal nation, despite being enemies, while George was just a mere colonial farmer, turned rebel. Whatever his views, Cornwallis's visit to Lafayette proved to be equally humiliating when he walked in to see James standing beside Lafayette.

Cornwallis huffed and snickered, "Ah, you rogue... then you have been playing me a trick all this time!"

After the war, James learned that his freedom would not be granted, and he returned to being William Armistead's slave servant. However, soon after, he met Marquis de Lafayette, who didn't forget James or his service to the war effort. As such, Lafayette drafted an impressive certification for his fellow soldier:

"This is to Certify that the Bearer By the Name of James Has done Essential Services to Me While I Had the Honour to Command in this State. His Intelligence from the Enemy's Camp were Industriously Collected and Most faithfully deliver'd. He perfectly Acquitted Himself With Some Important Commissions I Gave Him and Appears to me Entitled to Every Reward his Situation Can Admit of."

James petitioned the General Assembly to be granted his freedom and, despite some delays, was awarded his emancipation on January 1, 1787. It was then that James took on the surname of his honorable commander, thus becoming James Lafayette. Two years previously, in 1785, French artist Jean-Baptiste Le Paon painted a portrait of Marquis de Lafayette, and included presumably James by his side.

Meanwhile, James had settled in New Kent County, Virginia, and eventually purchased forty acres of land. Many years later, in 1824, James learned that Marquis de Lafayette was making a nostalgic visit to Yorktown. He wanted desperately to see his old commander again, but didn't have the finances to outfit himself for the long trip.

However, Lafayette happened to stop in Richmond, Virginia on his American tour and he spotted James standing in the crowd. The two briefly reunited, as a deep sense of camaraderie must have warmed their spirits.

Little else is known about James Armistead Lafayette, however he had petitioned the General Assembly one last time, requesting a pension for his military service. He promptly received $60 and then received $40 annually for the remainder of his life. James Armistead Lafayette lived another forty-seven years on his large tract of land as a free black man. He eventually passed away in Baltimore, on August 9, 1830. James Armistead Lafayette's daring spy craft and service to his nation, while not fully expecting his liberty in return, makes his endeavors all the more spectacular and admirable. That James did win his freedom in the end and lived a long life afterwards was compensation well deserved and well earned.

James Armistead Lafayette's covert tale may have been previously obscured for many years, but it has now taken its rightful place in the annals of American patriots.

The Author

Rich DiSilvio is an author of thrillers, mysteries, historical fiction and nonfiction. He has written books, historical articles, and commentaries for magazines and online resources. His passion for history, art, music, and architecture has yielded contributions in each discipline in his professional careers.

DiSilvio's work in the entertainment industry includes projects for historical documentaries, including James Cameron's *The Lost Tomb of Jesus, Killing Hitler, The War Zone* series, *Return to Kirkuk, Operation Valkyrie,* and cable TV shows and films such as *Tracey Ullman's State of the Union, Celebrity Mole, Blood Ties, Monty Python: Almost the Truth,* and many others.

He has written commentaries on the great composers (such as the top-rated Franz Liszt Site), and conceived and designed the Pantheon of Composers porcelain collection for the Metropolitan Opera, which also retailed throughout the USA and Europe.

His artwork and new media projects have graced the album covers and animated advertisements for numerous super-groups and celebrities, including, Pink Floyd, Yes, The Moody Blues, Cher, Madonna, Jay-Z, Willie Nelson, Miles Davis, the Rolling Stones, Alice Cooper, Queen, and many more.

As a software designer/developer, Rich pioneered the first interactive CD-ROM for educating staff and parents about Applied Behavioral Analysis (ABA) for training individuals with autism.

Rich lives in New York with his wife and has four children.

My Nazi Nemesis

GOLD AWARD WINNER

★★★★★ **"DiSilvio's plot is cunning and ingenious!"**
-- Jack Magnus for Readers' Favorite

A deadly love triangle launches a father and daughter team to hunt down a nefarious Nazi. Yet twists and turns abound, leading to a shocking climax.

Hardcover: 9780981762586
Paperback: 9780981762579
eBook: 9780981762593

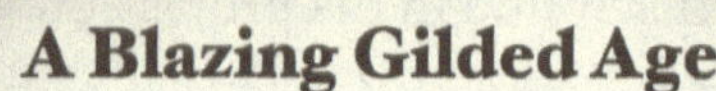

A Blazing Gilded Age

A riveting rags-to-riches saga about a poor family's struggle to survive amid a nation burning with ambition yet bleeding with injustice. Features, Teddy Roosevelt, JP Morgan, Mark Twain, Tesla and more.

Lauded by HISTORY/A+E and noted biographer Roger DiSilvestro.

Hardcover: 9780981762562
Paperback: 9780981762555
eBook: 9780997680720

Tales of Titans Series

Tales of Titans brings great historical figures to life with concise yet compelling essays, coupled with engaging narratives that enlighten readers to their miraculous deeds, and misdeeds, that have significantly shaped Western civilization.

This handsomely illustrated series offers readers brief biographical overviews and cogent analysis, while the quasi-fictional scenarios transport readers into a fascinating past, whereby putting flesh on the bones of several titans and offering glimpses into their hearts, minds, and actions.

Tales of Titans, Vol. I : From Rome to the Renaissance
Augustus & Livia, Vespasian & Titus, Hadrian, Constantine, Dante, Brunelleschi, Columbus, Vespucci, King Ferdinand, Pope Alexander VI & Cesare Borgia, and Leonardo da Vinci.

Tales of Titans, Vol. II: Renaissance to the Electro/Atomic Age
The Medicis, Gutenberg, Lorenzo de Medici, Savonarola, Leonardo & Machiavelli, Martin Luther, Queen Elizabeth I, Shakespeare, Galileo, Darwin, Marx, Stalin, Freud, Marconi, Edison, Tesla, Westinghouse, Einstein, Fermi and von Braun.

Tales of Titans, Vol. III: Founding Fathers, Women Warriors & WWII
Samuel Adams, Thomas Paine, George Washington, John Adams, Thomas Jefferson, James Madison, Alexander Hamilton, Ben Franklin, Sybil Ludington, James Armistead Lafayette, Elizabeth Cady Stanton, Susan B. Anthony, Harriet Tubman, Adolf Hitler, FDR & Churchill

Liszt's *Dante Symphony*

A historical mystery/thriller highlighting the belligerent rise of Nazi Germany from its Prussian roots, replete with ciphers, spies, murder and a stellar cast, including Albert Einstein, Rossini, Liszt, Nazi officers and Adolf Hitler.

Hardcover: 9780981762548
Paperback: 9780981762531
eBook: 9780997680713

The Winds of Time

The Winds of Time is a historical tour de force of Western civilization by Rich DiSilvio.

With masterful style, DiSilvio paints a fascinating historical canvas with the flare of a consummate artist. Key figures and the primary cultures that literally shaped the Western world are candidly analyzed, revealing both the dark and luminous sides of mankind. Moreover, DiSilvio's insightful essays add intriguing new dimensions to the historical record.

Hardcover: 9780981762524
eBook: 9780997680706

SILVER MEDAL WINNER

Meet My Famous Friends

Inspiring kids with Humor!
A whimsical picture book that pays homage to great historical figures in imaginative ways.

Author/Illustrator Rich DiSilvio presents a broad array of geniuses and heroes in a humorous and compelling fashion by altering their names and appearances, whereby making us see very familiar people in very different ways.

While children will get a kick out of looking at the comical artwork, teens and even adults will appreciate the witty play on words, inventive creations, and perhaps glean a thing or two about some of these iconic people who had a great influence on society in one form or another. Their lives and contributions have uplifted humanity in various ways, thus being great role models for young and old alike.

Hardcover: 9780997680751 Paperback: 9780997680768 eBook: 9780997680775

Danny and the DreamWeaver

A YA novelette by Rich DiSilvio (aka Mark Poe) about the power of dreams and the imagination.

When Danny meets Nostrildamus in his dream a bizarre journey begins!

Packed with dry humor, a mystery, and zany-looking artists, like Michelanjello & Hippopotamus Bosch, *Danny and the DreamWeaver* is an imaginative adventure of criminal intrigue and art history that demonstrates the importance of looking at life differently.

Paperback: 9780997680737
eBook: 9780997680744

Special Note to the Reader

Thank you for reading *Short Stories*

The Kennedy, Borgia, and Edison & Tesla vignettes presented here were first conceived between 2005 and 2009, and released in the Standard Edition of *The Winds of Time,* which featured a vast series of nonfictional essays and quasi-fictional narrative vignettes. The vignettes, however, were later replaced with pure nonfictional content to form the present Master Edition, which is still available. The remaining stories in this edition were written between 2014 and 2017.

It would be greatly appreciated if you take a moment to post a brief review about this book on your favorite retailer's website or social media forum, such as Amazon.com, barnesandnoble.com and goodreads.com.

Afterwards, send an email to info@dvbooks.net with the link to your review(s) and you'll receive **Special VIP Discounts** for other books.

www.ingramcontent.com/pod-product-compliance
Lightning Source LLC
LaVergne TN
LVHW091001080826
845145LV00003B/1087

9780998337548